MAR 23 2011

MYS

San Francisco, Paris, New York, Washington, Santa Fe

THE MISSING MOTHER

A Hallie Marsh Mystery

MERLA ZELLERBACH

firefall^{tm}

First Edition: November 2010

cover ilustration: Gladys Perint Palmer

ISBN: 9780915090525

FIREFALL EDITIONS
Canyon California 94516-0189

literary@att.net
www.firefallmedia.com

Novels by Merla Zellerbach

THE MISSING MOTHER

MYSTERY OF THE MERMAID

SECRETS IN TIME

Firefall Editions

RITTENHOUSE SQUARE

Random House

SUGAR

CAVETT MANOR

LOVE THE GIVER

THE WILDES OF NOB HILL

Ballantine

LOVE IN A DARK HOUSE

Doubleday

For Linda Zellerbach, my beautiful daughter-in-law, and the world's kindest and most caring physical therapist

It would be impossible to thank the many friends who have helped and encouraged me to write this book. My mentor/publisher Elihu Blotnick tops the list, my supportive husband, Lee Munson, my children and grandchildren, Gary, Linda, Laura and Randy Zellerbach.

Special thanks to nurse midwife Judith T. Bishop and Dr. Robert Liner, to Ingrid Nystrom at Books Inc., Elaine Petrocelli and Susan Leipsic at Book Passage, my brother, Dr. Sandor Burstein and wife Beth, Sen. Dianne Feinstein and Sir Richard Blum, my Chronicle buddies Leah (and Jerry) Garchik, Catherine Bigelow, Ruthe Stein and Carolyne Zinko, Nob Hill Gazette publisher Lois Lehrman, KGO radio Hall of Famer Ray Taliaferro, and "cover girl" Gladys Perint Palmer.

Inspiration came from many sources. Am grateful to Deputy D.A. Sharmin Bock, for her work on sex trafficking, to New York Times columnist Jane Brody and my dedicated co-workers at Compassion and Choices, to neighbors/mystery-lovers Judge Katherine Feinstein and Rick Mariano, and too, too many wonderful friends to name.

THE MISSING MOTHER

PART 1

— Chapter 1 —

Seattle, 2005

IF SEX WERE an Olympic sport, Sara Bowman mused, her brother Roger would walk off with the Gold. But maybe not this week.

She slowed her step to breathe deeply, the way her University of Washington Phys-Ed coach had taught her, then stopped at the street crossing. How the Seattle skyline glowed in the morning sunlight, sharp and crisp after a week of rain!

The storm had kept her from bicycling, fishing, waterskiing and all the outdoor sports she loved, but the skies had finally cleared, the trees sparkled with moisture, a rainbow crowned Lake Washington — and seven days of gloom were forgotten.

Five blocks later, Sara turned into a duplex and climbed the stairs to Roger Bowman's apartment. What a shame, she thought, that her oldest sibling might have to miss Christmas dinner with the family. Painting his hallway a few days ago, he'd fallen off a wobbly ladder and fractured his ankle – now encased in a twelve-inch cast.

Luckily, Roger's medical insurance paid most of the bills, and despite a pitch from his lawyer, he'd had no interest in suing the ladder company. Not only was it his own fault, he wisely reasoned that litigation would take hours of his time, money and negative energy. The family agreed with his decision, except for his middle brother, Andrew, who rarely agreed about anything.

"Is that you, Sis?"

She spoke into the box. "It ain't Britney Spears."

A buzzer admitted Sara and a second set of stairs delivered her to the front door. Finding it open, she walked into a bare hall and living room, furnished only with a desk and chair, a computer, a file cabinet and a bulging bookcase.

"I'm in the bedroom," called a voice. "I'm not alone."

"What a surprise." Untying her scarf, Sara shook out her long red hair, fluffed it with her hands, then lay her coat on the railing and hurried down the hall.

"Sure wish you'd get some furniture, Roger. This place has all the warmth of Death Row."

"Complaints, complaints." Roger Bowman pulled himself up in bed and smiled weakly. One leg was bent, the other was stretched out and elevated on pillows.

The sight of her strong, macho brother lying pale and helpless filled her with sympathy — an emotion she tried vainly to conceal. Despite a seven year age difference, she was closer to Roger than to either her middle brother, Andrew, or to Gary, the youngest.

People said she looked most like Roger, too. Both had deep blue eyes, ever-curious, and a bit too intense at times. Sara's skin was fair and soft with a pinkish glow, her features chiseled and delicate. Roger's nose was larger and wider, and supported dark-rimmed glasses. His beard and ponytail were more chestnut than red, and he wore them proudly.

Sara had no trouble understanding why women found him attractive — in a rumpled, sexy sort of way. Along with being half-owner of a successful software company, he had a bright, offbeat sense of humor, the ability to discuss almost any subject, and from all reports, a near-insatiable libido.

"Lookin' mighty sharp there, Sis. You didn't get all dressed up to pay a sick call. Where's the boyfriend?"

"Rick is where he always is, taking apart computers. I've been shopping — barely got out of Nordstrom with my life. Had to duck a hundred screaming kids waiting to see Santa. How do you feel?"

"Better than yesterday. Worse than tomorrow."

"You look better. Mom and Dad'll be over tonight. They said to ask what you need."

"Worship and adoration."

"You've got that — from yourself, anyway." She handed him a paper bag. "I brought you some literature."

He held up his gifts in surprise. "*Playboy? Hustler?* Who suggested these – the Marquis de Sade?"

"I thought you liked girlie mags."

"Not when I can't do anything about them. At the moment, my sex life's on hold — no pun intended."

"And your sex life is staying there!" A large, sturdy-looking woman in a white jumpsuit emerged from the bathroom carrying a pitcher of water. "I'm Linda, Roger's physical therapist — or as he says, his physical terrorist. You're Sis?"

"My brothers stuck me with that. Everyone else calls me Sara." She smiled. "Is your patient following orders?"

"You're kidding, right?" Linda straightened the covers and frowned. "Maybe you can convince him he's not Superman. He has to take it easy for a few weeks or he'll be in deep — uh, trouble."

"I see you know him well."

"I only met him yesterday, but I can write the script: physically active male forced to remain immobile while fracture heals. Becomes increasingly frustrated and irascible. Screams, bitches, drives everyone nuts. He'll feel better when he starts to move around. I came over to prepare him for crutches."

"You have to prepare? I thought you just got up and hopped away like the Easter bunny."

"That's funny, Sis."

"He's strong, so he probably *can* just hop away," said Linda. "But he'll need help negotiating the stairs. It can be tricky with an injury that doesn't bear weight." She turned to her patient. "I'll be back tomorrow. You won't be alone tonight, I presume?"

"Correct. A lady friend is coming over after work. Take my sister — please? I'm about to cork off."

"The pain medication makes him drowsy." Linda pulled up the blankets and tucked them around Roger's shoulders. "Don't forget your exercises."

"Yes, master," he mumbled.

"I've enjoyed our long visit." Sara kissed her brother's cheek. "Try to behave yourself."

"Like I have a choice…" His eyes closed as his head dropped to the side.

— Chapter 2 —

SURE I'M NOT making you late for something?" asked Sara.

Linda switched on the motor and smiled at her passenger. "You're only ten minutes away. How nice that you

11

live so close to your brother."

"It would be — except that he's always got some female in residence so I don't see much of him. But we email a lot. That's more than I do with my other brothers; they're both too busy. Andrew's twenty-eight, three years younger than Roger. He's a pediatrician like Dad and works in his office. He's married and they're about to have a baby. Gary's twenty-six and studying for the bar."

"You're the youngest?"

"Yup. I'm twenty-four — last of the brood. Dad says he was going to keep trying till Mom produced a girl." Sara chuckled. "The hardest part of growing up was realizing that the rest of the world doesn't spoil and protect you the way three older brothers do."

"I'm sure men still spoil you. You're pretty enough."

"Thanks, but it's a different world today. Women have gotten very aggressive and men have gotten so used to being chased, they just sit back and wait. The good men, I mean, like Roger. He never goes after women. They're always calling up and asking him out."

"Well, I'd never ask a man out. Would you?"

"I might — if I had theater tickets or something and he'd shown interest. I think it's great that we don't have to pretend to be the weaker sex anymore. You wouldn't believe how subservient my Mom is. She was brought up to think women are second class citizens."

"Not for me, they're not." Linda stopped at the red light. "Look at my field, health technology. Women are earning just as much as men. And this is 2005, forty years after 'Womens' Liberation.' "

Sara sighed. "I hope it's the same in my field. I just finished grad school and I'm studying to be a psychotherapist. My boyfriend tells me I'm great at listening to people's problems, but I'm a nut for exercise and I don't know how I'll manage sitting on my duff all day."

"Why don't you help people the way I do? You can use your psychology background and be physically active at the same time."

"What exactly do you do — besides visiting handsome men in their boudoirs?"

"Got time?"

"Sure."

Linda swung the car around. "I'll take you to the hospital and you can see for yourself."

— Chapter 3 —

ELLIOT BOWMAN, M.D., Ph.D., and a few other initials, lit his briar pipe, puffed several times and regarded his daughter anxiously. Sara's impulsiveness worried him almost as much as her need to keep up with her brothers. Andrew was born a bookworm, but Roger and Gary had always included Sara in their games and roughhousing. By age thirteen, she could climb a tree faster and put a better spin on a baseball than half the boys her age.

Now she was a woman — a beautiful young woman, as determined to succeed as her brothers were, and living with Rick Marino, a college dropout whose sole ambition was to tinker with computers. The best thing about their relationship was that they weren't married, and

Dr. Bowman fervently hoped, never would be.

"Suppose you tell us again, young lady. Yesterday you were planning to be a psychotherapist. This morning you met your brother's physical therapist, spent the day at the hospital and suddenly you're changing your whole life?"

"I'm not changing my life, Dad." Sara folded her napkin and set it by her plate. "All that's different is that instead of getting my degree in psych, I'll get it in PT — physical therapy — that is, if the department will accept me."

"No more psychology?"

"Linda, the woman who showed me around, said the hospitals *need* PT's with psychology training — it helps them deal with patients and their problems."

"What kind of problems, dear?"

Sara glanced across the table at her mother, white-haired and content. Her hands were busily needle-pointing a belt for one of her sons who would wear it every year for Christmas dinner, then return it to the back of his closet.

"Some patients have a hard time accepting their illnesses or disabilities, Mom. I'd teach them how to use their bodies after they've been sick or injured. Linda told me about physical modalities like electrical stimulation and traction that lessen pain and the need for heavy medication. The whole thing just feels right for me, Dad. Please don't try to discourage me."

"You haven't the vaguest idea what you're getting into." He set his pipe in the ashtray and fixed her sternly. "Physical therapy is much more than rehab. You'll be treating hopeless cases — people who've been in horrible accidents and have to live out their lives as paraplegics; people who've been maimed and burned and disfigured, people in constant pain, children who've been beaten and abused…"

"I don't expect it to be easy."

"You'll be dissecting cadavers."

"I can handle that."

"What about after your training? How crowded is the field? How many positions are available? What's the starting salary? Did you think to ask any of those questions?"

"Yes, I did. There are more jobs than there are people to fill them. The average salary's over seventy thousand. But Linda says I couldn't get into a program at this late date unless I had some pull. Dad…?"

The physician exhaled loudly and retrieved his pipe. Being a father wasn't easy — especially to a girl. His sons had listened to his advice, then gone off and done exactly as they pleased. They were strong-willed boys, loyal, loving and fiercely independent.

Sara, unfortunately, had learned from them. His efforts to talk her out of moving in with Rick two years ago had not deterred her in the slightest. Nevertheless, she was still his little girl and he felt strongly protective.

"Well, get me the information and I'll make inquiries," he said resignedly. "What does your boyfriend think of all this?"

"I haven't told him yet. You're super, Daddy."

Grinning with relief, she came around the table and kissed his forehead. "Aren't you going to see Roger? I told him you'd be over tonight."

"Oh, yes." Lottie Bowman stuffed the half-finished belt into her bag and stood up. "We are going over, aren't we, Elliot?"

"As soon as you're ready."

"I'll just get my coat and the banana bread. I hope I didn't burn it too badly. Sara, dear, did you ask him if he wanted anything?"

She laughed. "What Roger wants, Mom, I'm afraid you can't give him."

— Chapter 4 —

THANKS TO DR. Elliot Bowman's longtime friendship with a colleague, Sara was tested, interviewed, checked for possible criminal history, questioned about academic requirements, and finally accepted into Washington University's School of Medicine in St. Louis.

For the next two years, she worked and studied harder than she had ever dreamed possible. Occasionally, she wondered if she shouldn't have stayed with psychology, but she always came back to the fact that she enjoyed the challenges of her new career.

Helping patients in tangible ways — teaching them how to exercise and use equipment, "healing" them with her touch and her gentleness and her skills — this, she had learned, was immensely more gratifying than sitting in an armchair listening to them talk.

When she finally got her degree and passed her licensing exam in 2007, she ranked fourth in a class of nineteen women and five men.

Now, after a year of getting experience in the burn center of a small private hospital, she felt comfortable and competent in her profession. But it was time to move on.

— Chapter 5 —
November, 2008

RICK MARINO YAWNED, rubbed his eyes and turned over on his back.

"You awake?" whispered Sara.

"Yeah," he said, reaching over and pulling her to him. "How does it feel to be a free woman?"

She cuddled up in his arms. "I'm glad to leave that hospital, but I don't feel very free. I've got to decide where I'm going to work."

"Another hospital?"

"Yes, but a major one, with more challenges."

"Well, I'm taking in about seven grand a year. And if I get that job with Microsoft…"

"Rick," she said, drawing away to look at him, "You've been talking about working at Microsoft for months now and you haven't even gone for an interview. Roger offered to talk to you, too, and you haven't followed up. You don't seem very anxious to get a job."

"What's the hurry? I've got the rest of my life to be tied down."

"And you're perfectly willing to let me go on paying the rent — money we could be using for a down payment on a house?"

"Houses are for married people." His voice grew defensive. "And I'm not ready to marry."

"I wouldn't marry you anyway, when you don't have a job." She frowned and rested her head on one arm. They shared many of the same friends, a love of the outdoors, and a strong physical attraction. Her family didn't think he had any ambition, but she'd show them they were wrong. With her behind him, he could do anything — even open his own computer service shop.

Her voice softened. "I love you, Rick, and you say you love me. Don't you think it's time we began planning and saving for the future?"

"Sure I do, honey. I want to marry you." He drew her back to him. "But I don't want to be pushed into it. I'll know when I'm ready."

Damned if she was going to beg him. "Well, I might not be around when you are. My friend Dianne's going to California. She's got a job in Los Angeles that pays four thousand more than I'd be getting here."

"So what? You would never move away from your family."

"How do you know? I've always wanted to go to San Francisco."

He tilted her head to kiss her. "I know because I'm not moving anywhere and you're mad for my body. C'mere..."

"No – not now. I'm not in the mood."

"You will be. C'mere."

"No!" Jerking out of his grasp, she threw back the covers and climbed out of bed. "Sex isn't going to solve our problem, Rick. If you don't love me enough to get a job, I don't see much hope for us."

He sat up and fixed her curiously. "Is that some sort of ultimatum?"

She hadn't intended it to be, but he was challenging her the way her brothers used to challenge her and he was making her angry. "Call it what you will."

"Now hold on," he said, scowling. "I want a freakin' answer. Are you telling me I have to go out and look for a job this morning or we're through?"

His tone infuriated her. She turned to face him. Damn his good looks, she thought. Damn his suntanned face and broad shoulders and smooth, hairless chest. And damn the sexual hold he had over her. "All right, that's what I'm telling you."

"Don't be an asshole," he said wearily. "You and I have it made. We laugh, we have fun, we have a place to live and food to eat. What more do you want out of life? Problems? Pressures? Boredom?"

"I want stability. I don't think a career means much without a home and family."

"Anything else, Miss Princess? You want it all — love, romance, a home, a career, a family — what about the moon and the stars? Frankly, I'm tired of hearing what *you* want. What about what I want?"

"What do you want?"

"For now, I just want peace of mind. Is that too much to ask?" With a grunt, he rolled over on his side, slammed a pillow over his head and disappeared.

— Chapter 6 —

RICK WAS OUT of the apartment when Sara returned from her bike ride several hours later. Fresh air and exercise cleared her mind, and once she made a decision — even an impulsive one — she stuck to it.

Packing up her clothes and possessions, she piled them all in her car. With a heart full of sadness, she wrote Rick a note quoting Ecclesiastes — "There's a...time for everything..." and now was their time to be apart. She would be staying at her parents' house, then leaving shortly for California.

Several days later, after long chats and loving advice from big brother Roger, a teary scene with her mother and an emotional battle with her father who was torn between wanting her to dump Rick, but not wanting her to leave town, Elliot Bowman reluctantly drove his daughter to the airport.

The plane ride seemed longer than it was, as Sara dealt with guilt twinges about leaving Rick, who hadn't even called to say goodbye, damn him. There were even stronger guilt feelings for leaving her family a month before Christmas, along with the very real fear that she might be acting rashly.

Arriving in San Francisco late at night, she flirted with the temptation to catch a return flight home. Already, she missed her parents, her brothers, their lovely house on Lake Washington...

Anxiety almost got the better of her, but she was not

a quitter, she was not about to crawl back to Rick, and be-sides, it was time to make it on her own. The single suitcase she brought would hold her for now. Her mother would send her clothes once she was settled.

Money, however, would soon be in short supply. The small amount she'd saved had gone to pay the rent so Rick could stay in the apartment another month. Two thousand dollars from her father was all she had to live on until her first paycheck — assuming that she could talk herself into a job in a major hospital in a major city, without benefit of major hospital experience.

Affecting an air of confidence, she hailed a cab and remembered what she'd read in the guidebook. "Do you know the YMCA in Stonestown?"

"Yeah."

"Fine," she said, hauling her suitcase into the back seat. "Take me there."

PART 2

— Chapter 7 —

San Francisco, 2008

"SORRY TO DISTURB YOU, Dale, but Birdy's on the line and she sounds upset."

"Okay, thanks." Dale Redington quickly typed a few thoughts he didn't want to lose, then saved the work on his computer. "The phone," he mumbled, "is a boil on the ass of technology."

Ever since early that morning, when he'd gotten a call from his father, Walter Redington, CEO of the Redington Corporation, a large West Coast paper manufacturing company, he'd been toiling away, compiling a list of the pros and cons of acquiring a small paper mill in Oregon. Despite a degree in Economics from Amherst and a hard-earned MBA from Harvard, Dale had no desire to spend the rest of his life in the paper business. But how and when could he tell his father?

"Birdy's *waiting* for you, Dale. You're a big boy now. You can't treat her like she's still your nanny. Although — I could say you've gone to Idaho to rescue the Banbury Springs Limpet."

"The what?"

"It's a tiny aquatic snail with a spiral shell."

"Thanks, Miss Save-the-earth. I'll take the call."

Pausing a few seconds to mask his frustration at the interruption, he affected a cheerful voice. "Birdy, my love! Where've you been?"

"Waiting for you to divorce Daisy and marry me. Or maybe we could just live together?"

"Naah, you're too young for me. What's up?"

"Hate to bother you, but I need your help. Could you come by later?"

"It's important?"

"Yes."

"Then Redington to the rescue," he said, without hesitation. "I'll be there between three and four."

Driving to his destination, a small, two-bedroom house in San Francisco's mostly-middle-class Richmond district, Dale Redington was looking forward to seeing Birdy, his former nanny. He hadn't seen her since her birthday in May, and here it was almost Christmas.

Back in 1971, the year he was born, a full-time baby nurse had stayed long enough to teach him to walk, talk and use the potty. When she left, his mother hired Birdy (Roberta) Silbert, a pleasant, hard-working woman of twenty-two.

Dale was three at the time — and as Birdy liked to say, they "shared growing pains." (His mother later regretted not raising her only child herself.)

Thinking back to those years, Dale had many wonderful memories: Birdy schlepping him to the playground, to the movies, to his piano lessons, to his Judo classes, Birdy bribing him with Mars bars to do his homework, Birdy trying to explain the word "shtup" he learned from his friend, Rob Goldstein, Birdy catching him with a joint and not telling his parents, Birdy finding a condom in his pocket at age 13...and on and on.

Although she wasn't needed as a nanny once Dale reached his teens, the family loved Birdy and vice versa. Agreeing to work "temporarily" as maid, housekeeper, and cook on the chef's night off, she stayed with the Redingtons until osteoarthritis forced her to retire after 31 years. That was in 2005, when Dale's parents, Fran and Walter Redington, bought her a house and gave her a lifetime pension.

— Chapter 8 —

FINDING A PARKING place was a perennial problem in San Francisco, so Dale decided to pull into Birdy's driveway. Grabbing the pink azalea plant he'd picked up on the way, he hopped out of the car.

What could be so important it couldn't be discussed on the phone, he wondered. Money? Health problems? Her brother in jail again? Maybe she'd met a man at her church. At fifty-six, she wasn't too old to fall for the wrong guy.

Birdy was quick to answer the doorbell. Greeting Dale with a hug and a grin, she set the flowering plant on a table. "You know all my weaknesses, don't you. Thanks, darlin'."

He felt instant relief; she didn't seem upset. He did note that she was looking heavier. Perhaps the loose green top and dark slacks hid a few extra pounds, but she was far from obese. Her skin was wrinkled and reddish, a result of hours spent in the garden. Short gray hair, small brown eyes and a flat nose gave her a rather plain appearance.

"Vodka tonic?" she asked, leading the way into the living room.

"Thanks, Birdy, but Daisy's dragging me to some big party tonight, so I'd better hold off."

"Ah, yes." Daisy Redington was a subject Birdy preferred to ignore. Dale's Social-Registered wife had little

25

to gain by befriending her husband's old nanny — a fact Birdy had long ago noted and accepted.

Seeing, but not mentioning, the silvery streaks in his jet-black hair, she motioned to one of her two chintz-covered couches. "Have a seat, darlin'. I'll be right back."

"You've been buying out Tiffany again," he called after her, noting a shelf of cheap glass figures.

Moments later, she emerged from the hallway, no longer alone. Wrapped in her arms, in a pink woolly blanket, was a tiny sleeping baby.

Dale jumped to his feet. "Good Lord, Birdy — you've been busy!"

"She isn't mine — unfortunately."

"Whose is she?"

"That's what I want to talk to you about." The infant stirred, opened her eyes and seemed about to cry. Birdy was ready with a pacifier. "Hi, sweetheart," she cooed. "Here you go."

"What a beautiful little girl!" Dale peered cautiously. The baby dropped her plastic nipple just long enough to smile at him. Then her lips closed around it again. "I think I'm in love. What's her name?"

"Vicky — Victoria Snow. She's three months old. Her mother, Jenna Snow, lives next door. She left Vicky with me when she was only four weeks old. I've had her now for two months."

"Where's her mother?"

"That's the problem." Cuddling her precious bundle, Birdy sank down on the couch. Her eyes widened. "Darned if I know. I was only supposed to keep Vicky four days. Jenna's disappeared."

"Disappeared?" Dale stared back. "Where was she going?"

"To Los Angeles, for some reason. She'd been the associate editor at a small paper, the Golden Gate Star, for five years. But she took a two-week leave a year ago, in December. She found out she was pregnant and for some reason, didn't want anyone to know."

"She never went back to work?"

"That's right. And she didn't even let them know she wasn't coming back. A few weeks ago, a woman from the Star finally got around to come looking for her. She rang my bell and asked if I knew where she was."

"What'd you say?"

"That I thought she was living with her family back east. I didn't want them reporting her missing because I knew she was home all those months awaiting her baby and trying to keep it a secret. She's only been really missing for the last two months, after she left Vicky with me."

"What did the woman say when she heard Jenna was back east?"

"She said they still had a lot of her stuff. She asked me to come in and pick it up, so I did. Mostly junk — papers, books, files. It's all piled up in my breakfast room. There's even more in her office next door."

"What about her family back east?"

"I made that up. Jenna had no close relatives. She was an only child. Her parents were dead. She loved her husband, Shane, but he wasn't very demonstrative. She used to wear his picture in a silver locket. Told me she never took it off, not even to shower or go swimming."

"Where's Shane now?

Birdy shook her head. "He died of a heart attack last December. Never even knew his wife was pregnant. That's when she took a leave from work, to get their affairs in order. But as I said, she didn't go back to her job. She just stayed home, not wanting anyone to know she was pregnant, or even that she was there. She spent hours working on her laptop."

"What was she working on?"

"Who knows? She was always interested in subjects she couldn't do much about, like sex trafficking, domestic abuse, serious problems. And she insisted on giving birth to Vicky at home, with a midwife. After Vicky was born, she stayed home for another four weeks and never took her out of the house."

"Not even to a doctor?"

"Nope. Fortunately, except for a little croup, Vicky's very healthy."

Dale nodded. "That's a weird story. Why wouldn't Jenna want anyone to know she had a baby?"

"Beats me. But she begged me not to tell people."

"Have you been inside the house?"

"Sure, I go there to get things for Vicky all the time. The mail and bills are piling up."

"Is Jenna's laptop or computer there?"

"I looked everywhere, but I couldn't find it."

"Hmmm. Where's your phone? We have to file a missing person's report."

"Oh, no! Please? That's why I called you. They'll

take Vicky away, put her in the system and give her to some awful foster parents. I won't let them ruin the life of this beautiful child!"

Dale groaned. "Damn it, Birdy, I haven't time to argue. We'll have to call the police sooner or later. Give me a day to think this over. Do you have enough money for Vicky's needs?"

"Yes, thanks, we're fine. I — just don't know what to do."

"Don't do anything. Who knows about this?"

"Nobody. I don't talk to anyone."

"That's wise. Jenna's behavior suggests she was worried about Vicky's safety, and possibly her own. Wait for my call and we'll figure out our next move. Okay?"

"Okay." The older woman wiped a tear. "I know I'm a pain in the butt."

"Yes, but you're my pain in the butt." With a hug and a peck on her cheek, Dale rolled his eyes to himself and hurried out the door.

— Chapter 9 —
2008

THE STARTLING FLASH of the camera made Dale Redington wince. He hadn't seen the photographer approach, nor had he realized that his wife had momentarily left the dance floor to come back to their table.

"Can we get you two together, Mr. R.?"

"Not now, please."

"Oh, don't be such a party poop!" Daisy Redington

patted her blond waves into place, leaned toward her husband and brightened into a smile. It was pretty and perfect, an absolute nothing of a smile.

"That's it — beautiful!" The futility of trying to snap a reluctant husband was familiar to the cameraman, so he concentrated on his willing subject, shooting her from several angles. "Thanks, Daisy. I think I've gotten all the people you wanted. If there's nothing else —"

"Oh, Scotty, you're a doll. Did you get the orchids by the entrance?"

"Yes. I've taken about 150 shots. I'll post them on the web next week."

"But no, sweetie, I promised the Chronicle you'd send the jpegs right over, in time for the Sunday edition."

"I don't think –"

"Oh, Scotty, just for me? Don't you remember we talked about this?"

The photographer hoisted a leather case over his shoulder and cussed silently. He had no recollection of a discussion and no one told him he'd be up all night. "Okay," he said, with a sigh. "But I'll have to send them as is. No time for touch-ups or labels."

"You don't need labels. Catherine and Carolyne know everyone in town."

Daisy turned away as the man hurried off. "Dale, honey, would you hand me my purse? I need lipstick."

"No. It's after one and we're going home."

She stared at her husband in surprise. "I know you're tired, dear, but I can't leave as long as we still have guests. I'm chair of this event, remember?"

"Yes, I remember." Dale glanced about the Court of Honor leading into the Palace of the Legion of Honor — a handsome Beaux Arts Museum overlooking the Pacific Ocean. San Francisco's premium caterer, Paula McCall, had constructed a huge white tent over the outdoor courtyard surrounding Rodin's famous sculpture, *The Thinker*.

Underneath the temporary roof, forty round tables seated more than 400 guests, all of whom had paid a minimum of $1,500 to support the arts, dine, dance, see and be seen.

Dale's patience was dissolving. "Do you realize we left home at five this afternoon? We've been 'partying' for more than eight hours!"

"I know that, sweetie, and I'm exhausted. Do you have any idea the kind of time and effort it takes to put on the Holiday Gala? It's like the Opening of the Opera and the Symphony combined!"

"I do know. I haven't had a wife for ten months. I've had a two-legged committee with a cell phone for a head." He pushed away his heart-shaped raspberry mousse. "You can do what you want, Daisy. But don't insist on dragging me to any more of these affairs. I've had it! Are you coming home or not?"

"I can't leave yet."

"Then take a cab." He rose and headed for the exit.

"Dale, wait!" she called. "The band's just finishing. Give me ten minutes to tie up loose ends."

"Ten it is, then I leave."

— Chapter 10 —

AS DALE WAITED, checking his watch every few minutes, he glanced about the tent, noting for the first time, the holly branch centerpieces, the potted fir trees with their gleaming ornaments, the bright red tablecloths. A handful of penguin-suited gents and sleek-gowned ladies swayed to the last strains of a Beatles' song whose name he couldn't remember.

Watching Daisy scurry across the floor in her stiletto heels, he thought how well her slim figure fit into her green beaded dress — encasing her too tightly for his taste — but Daisy no longer seemed to care what he liked.

Strange how time affected relationships. For no reason, his mind shot back fifteen years to that night in 1993 when he first met Daisy deWilte at Ann Townsend's "coming out" party.

Ann had introduced them with the line, "You two should have a lot in common. Her great-great grandmother was a Bradstreet." The credit hadn't impressed him. One of her ancestors belonged to a British publishing family and his family sold newsprint. Big deal.

Yet he'd been instantly attracted to the pretty nineteen-year-old. Perhaps it was the golden-blond locks pulled back off her face into a single long braid. Perhaps it was her upturned nose that crinkled like an accordion when she laughed. More likely, it was those firm young breasts that threatened to break loose of their casings and pop out of her pink chiffon bodice at any perilous second.

Three years her senior, tall and even-featured, with

dark, soulful eyes and a head of curly black hair, Dale Redington was one of the town's most eligible bachelors. After Harvard Business School, he'd returned to join the family-controlled company — a vast concern of timber forests and paper mills, with headquarters in San Francisco.

The couple's courtship was brief. They'd only been dating three months, when Daisy tearfully announced her pregnancy. Assuming the entire blame, Dale did what a responsible young man should do, and four weeks later, their very social wedding was splashed across the pages of *Town & Country*. James deWilte Redington, nine pounds, eleven ounces, entered the world "prematurely" seven months after the ceremony.

"I'm ready to go, Dale."

His wife's voice returned him to reality. "Good!"

"But I have to keep my coiffure for tomorrow and it's blowing a gale. Would you be a sweet angel and get the car?"

"Okay." He helped her into her sable jacket, wondering why she still wore furs. At the same time, he silently reaffirmed his vow to himself: no more galas, no more openings. "Wait for me in front."

— Chapter 11 —

THE SIDEWALKS were dark and deserted several minutes later, as the pale blue Jaguar emerged from the Sea Cliff district onto Lake Street. Daisy checked the lock on her door and cuddled into her fur. "It's awfully quiet at this hour. Could you get over to California Street?"

"Sure. When the opera opening comes around next year, you'll have your own car. You can go home whatever way you please."

She stared curiously. "What do you mean?"

"Just what I said. From now on, you can drag one of your 'escorts' to the pre-opera cocktail party and the pre-opera supper, and the intermission parties, and the post-opera ball and all the other opening night clown acts. I'm bowing out."

"But Dale, you've been going with me for years. Why suddenly...?"

"It's not sudden. It's because I've learned to dislike this whole sophomoric competition to see who can show off the most elaborate gowns, who can get the most pictures taken, who's snagged the biggest celebrities for their box. The men sit there half-asleep, wishing they were home watching TV, and the women are all so busy trying to figure out what each others' gowns cost, they might as well be listening to a street singer."

"That's not so. Lots of people love opera."

"Yes, but they're not the ones who attend the opening. Those performers on stage are superb artists. They've struggled and studied and dedicated their lives to perfecting their art. And I resent being part of an audience that's too boozed-up, too ignorant and too self-involved to appreciate them."

Daisy took a moment to think; she could only push him so far. "Well, the patrons may not all be opera fans, but they do look forward to a glamorous, exciting evening. Without their money and support, there wouldn't *be* any opera. Say — I thought you were getting out of this district."

"Okay, okay." He turned onto a side street. "Daisy, you know that..." Stopping mid-sentence, he stared through the windshield. "What the hell?"

Daisy's eyes darted to a small shingled house, one of several look-alike homes on the block. Flames shot out of a second story window, sending up billows of black smoke.

Almost without thinking, Dale pulled over to the curb, dialed 911, gave the address, then grabbed a flashlight.

"Where are you going?" asked Daisy.

"Someone might be in there."

"You're leaving me all alone?"

"Lock the car. You'll be safe. The fire department's on the way."

"Dale, don't desert me!" She clutched his arm. "I'm a sitting duck with all this jewelry."

"Then take it off!"

Twisting out of his coat, he left her holding his jacket, slammed the door and ran toward the building. As he reached the entrance, a young Asian woman came stumbling out, rubbing her eyes. "Please, sir! My grandpa's up there and he's so stubborn, he won't move. He keeps rambling about 'moral purification' or something and says Buddha will save him."

"Wait here." Bounding up the stairs three at a time, Dale found a locked door and banged on it. "Open up, Grandpa!" Getting no answer, he kicked a hole through the thin wood, then reeled back as the stench of burning flesh engulfed him. Shoving his hand through the opening, he flipped the bolt and entered.

Thick clouds of smoke blurred his vision as he sidestepped the charred carcass of a dog. A man's voice moaned weakly from behind a wall of flames. Holding his breath and using his right arm as a shield, Dale dashed through the fire to where a small panicked figure stood cowering in a corner. "Come on, Pops, we're getting out of here!"

A trembling hand raised in protest. "No, no! You not friend —"

"No time to argue." Gripping the man's armpits, he dragged him back through the flames, protecting him with his own body. Half-blinded by smoke, and gagging from the gases, he hoisted the man on his shoulder, tottered down the stairs and out to a patch of lawn. Dropping him on the grass, he rolled him over on his stomach to douse the fire, then rolled him back again.

Instinct and adrenaline carried Dale another few seconds until he realized, with a shriek of recognition, that his own hair and shirt were on fire. Staggering towards the curb, he took a few dazed steps, then crumpled to the ground. A woman screamed, sirens screeched, and suddenly, everything went black.

— Chapter 12 —

"WE'RE SORRY TO TROUBLE you at this time, Mrs. Redington." Two men had entered the emergency waiting room. One carried a BlackBerry and a notebook, the other, a camera.

Daisy set down her magazine. "It's all right. Are you — ?"

"We're from the Chronicle." The reporter introduced himself and his photographer. "Do you think you could tell us what happened?"

"I'll try," she sighed. "Dale and I were driving home from the Holiday Gala — it's a major benefit for the Opera and the Symphony. We do it every year in late November. I was the chair and I was exhausted. Well, as I said, we were driving home when we saw flames coming out of this house and I told Dale to stop."

Tears filled her eyes. "He insisted I stay in the car. Next thing I knew, he was stumbling out of the building carrying this poor old man. They were practically human torches!"

"Do you mind?" asked the photographer, focusing his camera on her.

"I guess it's okay…nothing really matters now, except — well, Dale's always had this crazy hero complex. The greater the danger, the more he seems to like it. He rolled that old gentleman over and over on the lawn to put out his flames and didn't realize he was on fire himself."

"What did you do?" asked the reporter.

"I jumped out of the car and tried to smother his flames with my coat." Well, she would have done so, had the ambulance not arrived at that moment. "The drivers — oh, God, it was horrible. Part of his skin —" She paused for composure. "They put something over his mouth and took him off on the stretcher."

"Where is he now?"

"Inside the Emergency Room. They wouldn't let me go with him."

"What about the man he rescued?"

"The firemen said he didn't make it."

The photographer's voice was hesitant. "Okay to snap you, Mrs. Redington?"

"Well, Dale's the real hero. But I don't mind. I know you have to go back with a picture."

The bulb flashed and the man packed away his camera. The reporter stepped forward. "Are you up to a few questions?"

"Short ones."

"How old is Mr. Redington?"

"Thirty-seven."

"And you have a son?"

"Jimmy's fourteen. He's home sleeping — oh, God, here's the doctor." She hurried across the room. "How's my husband?"

The man in the white coat nodded reassurance. His face was expressionless, his voice mechanical. People became that way after a few weeks in the Emergency Room, or people couldn't stand what they saw.

"He'll pull through, Mrs. Redington. He has serious burns — on his upper torso, his right arm and the right side of his face. We've called your family physician, Dr. Harris, as you requested. He's on his way."

"Thank goodness!" Daisy breathed a sigh. "Where is my husband, Doctor? Can I see him?"

"No, I'm sorry. Our trauma team is busy monitoring his vital functions, administering vaccines and antibiotics and trying to determine the extent of his injuries. I'm sure Dr. Harris will discuss everything with you when he gets here — including the surgery."

"Surgery?"

"Yes, he'll need skin grafts. Now, if you'll excuse me —"

"Do you know anything about the man he rescued?" interrupted the reporter.

"Chinese-American male, around seventy, DOA — dead on arrival. He suffered laryngeal occlusion caused by inhalation of toxic fumes, and possible MI — myocardial infarction due to severe coronary disease."

"He had a bad heart."

"Yes. We talked to his physician. He wouldn't have lived six months."

"How sad," muttered Daisy. Dale's efforts were hardly worth it.

The doctor eyed her coolly. "I suggest you go home now, Mrs. Redington. Perhaps you can get some sleep. Your family will need you to be strong. I'll have Dr. Harris call you as soon as he's seen your husband."

The patronizing tone annoyed Daisy. But this was no time for a scene. "That's fine, thanks for your help."

She tightened the belt of her sable coat, hoping the reporters wouldn't notice that it bore no ravages of its alleged rescue mission. Then she turned to them. "It's very dark outside. Would one of you gentlemen be kind enough to walk me to my car?"

— Chapter 13 —
Later That Morning

FRANCES "FRAN" REDINGTON, short and petite, pale and tight-lipped, grabbed the arm of a passing nurse. "My son Dale's in there, in the Burn Center. Would you please tell me why I can't go in?"

The nurse jerked away. "I'm sorry, Ma'am. This isn't my floor. You'll have to ask at the desk."

"Try to be patient, Nana." The lanky, dark-haired teenager patted his grandmother's shoulder and spoke softly. "Remember, Dr. Harris warned us that Dad's all bandaged-up like a mummy."

"How 'bout a chair, dear? If we're going to wait, let's go to the waiting room." Walter Redington started down the hall.

"I don't want a chair, Walter. What time is it?"

The white-haired man in the pin-striped suit turned and walked back. He was calm and quiet-spoken, and carried himself with authority. "It's ten to eleven, almost lunchtime. I wonder what happened to Daisy."

"She hadda go down to the newspaper." Jimmy Redington tried to mask his feelings, but his mother's absence distressed him. "Somethin' about the gala last night. She said a lot of people were countin' on her."

No surprise, thought Fran. That dizzy daughter-in-law wouldn't visit her own mother in the hospital if it meant missing a chance for publicity.

Fran and Walter Redington had often discussed their amazement that their grandson, Jimmy, had turned out so well, despite the fact that Daisy rarely had time for him — or perhaps, because of it.

Once, Fran had even tried talking to Daisy — telling of her own regrets that she'd let Birdy raise Dale instead of doing it herself. But Daisy had had no interest in scaling down her volunteer efforts. They brought her what money alone could never buy — praise, popularity and public recognition.

"Got plans for the weekend, Jimmy?"

"Not serious ones, Gramps. Dad and I were goin' hikin' today."

"Maybe you could go with a friend. There's nothing you can do sitting around here."

Jimmy shook his head. Tall for his fourteen years, he bore a strong resemblance to his father. "It wouldn't be any fun without Dad."

No sooner had he spoken than the thick, double doors opened and Dr. Hadley Harris appeared. His face was drawn, his eyes sad and tired. "Fran — Walter — Jimmy: Dale will recover, but it's going to be a long, painful process. He'll need all the love and understanding you can give him."

"Is he in pain?" Fran's voice was anguished.

"He's heavily sedated, so no, he's not suffering. I've ordered as much painkiller as he needs. We were lucky to get him in here this morning. This is one of the three top burn centers in the country."

"Who's in charge?" asked Walter.

"Dr. Mitchell Cummings, a brilliant plastic surgeon who specializes in burn reconstruction. I promise you

41

Dale is getting the best care he can get."

"Is Dad awake?"

"Yes and no. He drifts in and out."

Walter's brow wrinkled. "The prognosis, Hadley?"

"I think we can be hopeful. He'll have normal vision in his left eye, eventually in both eyes, and full use of his left arm. Probably his right, too, but it will take some doing. He's a lucky guy. His vital organs weren't affected, so the immediate problem is to keep the bacteria from invading the exposed flesh on his chest and right arm."

Fran bit her lips. "His face?"

"He'll have some disfigurement, but Mitch is the best in the business. The important thing is for Dale to have complete rest and give his body a chance to use its own healing powers. Tell Daisy absolutely no callers —" He glanced around. "Where *is* Daisy?"

"She'll be here," said Fran, not hiding the frustration in her voice. "May we go in now?"

"Yes." He handed them sterile paper gowns and shoe covers. "Put these on. Hospital rules. Don't touch *anything*. No physical contact with anyone inside the unit, especially the patient. Bacterial contamination could be a death warrant to Dale." He paused a moment, then added, "And for God's sake, sound upbeat!"

His manner was calm as he took Fran's arm and led the family into the burn center, a separate, specialized unit on the fifth floor of St. Paul's Hospital. They walked past a long, Formica-topped nursing station where a young woman in a blue smock sat typing at a computer. A few steps beyond, Dr. Harris pointed to a set of cranes and pulleys suspended over a table that looked like a large strainer.

"That's the treatment area, where the patients are cleansed. The room is kept very warm, the patient lies naked on the table and the tech sprays him with a handheld shower. The water drains off and we redress his wounds." He turned the knob to a private room. "And here we are."

Dale lay motionless under a sheet, his head elevated and his chest swathed in dressings. His right arm was encased in a stocking-like support that held it vertical. A narrow feeding tube poked out of his nose; clear fluid drained into his left arm.

Jimmy swallowed hard. Fran gasped as her husband moved to support her. When she finally spoke, her voice was strong and optimistic. "It's your mother, darling. We're proud of what you did, but not very happy to see you this way. Can you hear me under those bandages?"

"Y-yes." Dale's murmur was low, almost unintelligible. "I'm — fine, Moth'r."

"Hi, Dad. Can I borrow a sport jacket tonight?" Jimmy knew his father well. The last thing he wanted was pity.

The patient's head moved slightly. "B-big date, Jimbo?"

"Nope, I was just kiddin'. Randy's comin' over and we're goin' to the movies. How do you feel?"

"Okay —- c-consid'ring the alter'tive."

"You sure don't look okay. Mom had to do somethin' real important but she'll be here any minute. Gramps is here."

Dale tried to raise his left arm. "S-sorry…"

"Don't talk, son. Save your strength." Walter started to reach for his hand, then remembered the doctor's warning. No physical contact. No emotion. No fumbling speech. "Don't worry about the office. We can handle things till you get back. All that matters is for you to get well."

"Wha' happ' to man?"

"Man?" asked Walter.

"Maybe he means the man he rescued." Jimmy looked to his grandmother, who nodded firmly. It was all right to tell the truth. "He didn't make it, Dad, he had a bad heart. Apparently, he fell asleep and dropped a lit cigarette, an' that's what started the fire. But everyone's sayin' you're a hero for tryin' to save him. The Chronicle has a picture of you and Mom at the party last night. I'm gonna be a real big shot at school."

"D- dot the 'I'."

"What's he saying?" asked Fran.

Jimmy blushed. "Private joke."

"That's enough talking for now." Hadley Harris pulled the curtain around the bed. "I'm scooting your family out of here, Dale. If you need anything for pain, squeeze the buzzer in your left hand. A psychiatrist will be dropping by to ask you a few questions — routine procedure. I'll be back this evening."

No sound came from the bed.

"Is he sleepin'?" whispered Jimmy.

"Looks that way." Dr. Harris motioned towards the hall. "Take the back elevator and you'll avoid the reporters.

44

Security has orders not to let anyone up here."

"Thanks, Hadley." Walter extended his hand.

"No thanks needed, old friend. Have your mother call me when she gets home, Jimmy."

"Yeah — sure." His voice faltered as he murmured, "She musta had trouble with the car."

PART 3

— Chapter 14 —

November, 2008

AFTER SPENDING her first night, Friday, at the San Francisco YMCA, Sara Bowman checked the newspaper rental announcements, then answered a Craigslist ad for a woman to share a Sacramento Street apartment in Pacific Heights, an upscale residential district.

Landlady Hallie Marsh, she discovered, was warm and friendly. The pretty, slim blonde was a bit older, perhaps in her early thirties, and owned Hallie Marsh Communications, a public relations firm. She worked long days, and as she quickly told Sara so there would be no misunderstanding, spent ninety-nine percent of her time with a "tall, prematurely gray and sinfully handsome" journalist named Dan Casserly, whom she called "Cas."

The room in the apartment was small, tastefully furnished and immaculate, the rent higher than Sara had planned to pay, but she shared Hallie's dislike of dirt and clutter. The neat, low-maintenance abode appealed to her, as did Hallie's no-nonsense approach to life, and she'd said yes on the spot.

With so few personal belongings, settling in was easy, and the next morning, Sara rose early to walk in the fog. The rest of the day she spent visiting major hospitals, leaving her résumé and whenever possible, talking to someone on the staff. After four interviews, she felt optimistic about three of them. But a week passed with no response — until the phone rang early Saturday morning.

As Sara lay in bed thinking about the call, a noise at the front door gave her a start. Instinctively, she threw off the covers and grabbed her robe. "That better be you, Hallie!"

"Citizens for Decency," announced a female voice. "Get that man out of your bed!"

"I wish," Sara mumbled, tying her sash as she stumbled down the hallway.

Hallie was already in her room, removing a garment bag from her closet. "I need a change of clothes. What are you doing up so early? It's not even seven."

Sara rubbed her eyes. "I could sleep till noon. But I got an SOS call at six-thirty. I'm due at St. Paul's Hospital at nine."

"A job?"

"I'm hoping. I spoke briefly with Dr. Cummings, who runs the Burn Center, a few days ago and he seemed encouraging. Good-looking, too."

"Oh?"

"With a gold wedding ring — and an ego the size of Texas."

"Maybe he has body parts to match," teased Hallie.

Sara frowned. "You're looking at someone who has no desire to find out. Anyway, he had his PT — physical therapist — manager call me. She made sure I had burn experience, then she asked if I could come in today. Apparently, they have some new VIP patient and most of their PT's are off for the weekend."

"Good for you — and good luck!"

Hallie disappeared to rummage through a desk in her office, leaving Sara to ruminate on how little she knew about her new housemate. Besides the basics, all Hallie had told her was that she'd married at nineteen, divorced four months later, survived breast cancer and a double mastectomy, and had recently met this divine man, Cas, aboard a cruise ship.

But then Hallie didn't know much about her, either, except for her job references.

Wrapping her bathrobe still tighter, Sara headed for the kitchen, then filled a mug with instant hot water. Dipping in a tea bag, she glanced at the clock, then opened the morning Chronicle. A headline caught her eyes: "Redington Heir Badly Burned in Heroic Rescue."

The front page showed a picture of a couple in formal attire. The man was well-built and attractive, with dark, wavy hair — but he looked as if he'd rather be swimming with sharks. The woman was blonde, beautiful, and beaming as if she'd just won an Oscar (de la Renta, perhaps).

The caption read: "Paper heir Dale Redington and wife, Daisy, as they arrived at the Legion of Honor last night. En route home, Mr. Redington stopped at a fire scene to rescue an elderly man. The victim died and Redington was rushed to Golden Gate Emergency, then transferred to the Burn Center at St. Paul's Hospital. He remains in serious but stable condition. Story on page four."

Sara flipped to the long article — starting with a description of the rescue, followed by a history of the "hero's" family business. The Redington Corporation, she read, was founded in San Francisco in 1924 by Aaron James Redington, and had grown to be one of the country's largest paper manufacturers.

Farther down the article were pictures of Daisy and Dale's very social marriage — he looked happier there — plus descriptions of the family's many philanthropic and civic accomplishments.

So that was the VIP getting all the attention at St. Paul's Burn Center!

"Hey, who's the hunk?" Hallie reappeared and stared over Sara's shoulder. "Redington, huh? Too bad he's married. I'll bet that's why St. Paul's called you — they need a good-looking broad to stave off the reporters."

"Thanks for your confidence in my skills."

"Well, I'm sure they checked your references, but it doesn't hurt that you look the way you do. Has anyone warned you that this city's no paradise for single women?" Hallie didn't wait for an answer. "But what city *is* these days? How's a girl supposed to know if a guy's got Herpes or Gonorrhea or Chlamydia? Or even AIDS? That's enough to scare anyone celibate."

"What brought that up?"

"Just want you to be aware. Those horny young interns at the hospital will be all over you. And watch out for those doctors whose wives don't understand them. Good luck, Miss Newly-employed. I'm off to earn my daily croissant."

— Chapter 15 —
Two days later

"PAGING DR. CUMMINGS. Dr. Mitchell Cummings."

"What now?" The physician pulled the stethoscope out of his ears and scowled. Reaching for his cell phone, he listened a moment, spoke a few brisk words, clicked off and bent down over his patient. "Sorry, Dale. I tell the switchboard not to bother me unless it's an emergency, but it doesn't seem to register. The good news is that your lungs are clear. How do you feel?"

Dale Redington lay motionless on his back, a feeding tube in his nose, an intravenous line still infusing fluids into his veins. "Chilly," he murmured.

"That's normal. Body heat escapes through the burn. I'll turn up the heat shield — that's the overhead screen that gives off warm air. How's the pain?"

"Mostly in the arm — chest."

"What about hoarseness? Soreness in the throat?"

"No."

"You're lucky; there's no respiratory involvement. If all goes well, we'll start skin grafting day after tomorrow."

"Is it — necessary?"

"Yes. Otherwise, you won't heal." He turned his patient's head on the pillow. "Try to relax if you can. You'll feel a slight discomfort."

With sterile, gloved hands, Mitch carefully peeled away the face dressings until the charred skin lay exposed. "You're looking better. I'm going to apply some anti-bacterial ointment."

Dale winced under the doctor's touch.

"Easy now — another minute more. There, it's all done."

"When — can I see?"

"The ophthalmologist wants to keep your eyes patched a few days longer. I know it's hard lying there in the dark, but your corneas need time to heal. Think of it as insurance for your vision. Now, what do you need?"

"A new body?"

Mitch smiled. "There's plenty of mileage left on the old one. Rest quietly for a few minutes, Dale, then we're going to start the tub treatment. It won't be fun, but you're getting something for the pain. Your doctor, Hadley Harris, will be there to supervise."

"Thanks — I think."

A nurse in a surgical cap and mask stepped through the doorway as Mitch was about to leave. "We all set, Doctor?"

"As soon as Dr. Harris arrives."

"Yes, of course. I'll just check the IV."

Mitch strode across the floor to the nursing station where the object of his search stood with her back to him, scanning the patients' charts. Sara Bowman had only been at the hospital two days, but the staff liked her, patients had already started asking for her, and he — well, his eyes took in every fold of her blue scrubs. Mentally, he undressed her — and the image aroused him.

" 'Morning, Sara. Could I see you in my office?"

She spun around, catching the lust in his eyes before he had time to mask it. "Good morning, Dr. Cummings. Now?"

"Yes. It's about Mr. Redington."

I'll bet, she thought, as she followed his brisk walk down the hall. Mitch's randiness was a favorite topic among the female staff. A vague smile crossed her lips as she recalled the notice someone had posted on the nurses' bulletin board: *Ladies! Want a good time? Call Ext. 291. Fast, energetic service by able 40-year-old. No strings attached."*

Apparently, a curious nurse had called Extension 291 and when the surgeon answered, reported the hoax. To Mitch's credit, he'd laughed aloud before telling the nurse to take it down.

"I hear good things about you, Sara," he said.

"Thank you." She glanced sideways. The square jaw, light brown hair and intense green eyes that some women found irresistible, held not the slightest interest for her. "And you've a good tan. Been out in the sun?"

"That hour on the deck yesterday must've paid off." He opened the door to his office and closed it behind him. "You should see my terrace. It looks down on Sausalito and the bay. On a clear day you can see all the way across the Golden Gate Bridge. Then San Francisco spreads out like a fantasyland."

"Does your wife enjoy it, too?"

"She's never there. It's my place. Have a seat. Ellen and I respect each other's needs to have separate friends and interests. That's the only way a marriage can work."

"You're lucky. Some husbands say their wives don't understand them. Yours seems to understand you very well."

"She does." Her sarcasm escaped him. "And I'm serious. My view is extraordinary — far better than anything you've got in Seattle."

"I'll take your word for it." Folding her arms, she sat down and faced him across a neat, organized desk. His office was small, yet handsomely appointed with Roman shades, thick brown carpet and top-of-the-line McGuire furniture. Gold-framed diplomas and a signed lithograph decorated the walls, but nary a picture of his wife or two sons. "Now — what about Mr. Redington?"

"He gets VIP treatment, all the way. He gets whatever he wants, whenever he wants it. The Frances and Walter Redington Foundation gives away millions each year to deserving causes. With a mere pittance of that largesse, I could get enough matching funds from investors to build my own plastic surgery clinic." He searched her face for a change of expression. There was none.

"I've been dreaming about this for a long, long time," he continued, "and wondering whom I could approach. Then the Lord came along and dropped Mr. Dale Redington right into our laps." He stared at her meaningfully. "And I do mean 'our'. There'll be a place for you in my clinic, Sara. I've watched you work and I'm impressed. I could use someone with your talents. How does Administrative Assistant sound?"

"Premature."

"Don't be so certain. In any case, I'm counting on you to see that Dale and all members of his family have nothing but the highest praise for our unit and everyone in it. Get my meaning?"

"Subtlety is not your greatest asset."

"I particularly want you to look after him," he went on, ignoring her gibe. "I want you to comfort him during the debridement and spend as much time with him as you can, as if you were his private nurse. I've already talked to your supervisor and left orders at the desk that you're to be his physical therapist, his psychologist, and his soul mate."

"What about the other patients?"

"He comes first. If we have to, we'll add another PT. The senior Redingtons wanted to hire round-the-clock nurses for Dale, but I said they'd only need them for the night shifts. You'll be there during the day, and there's nothing like a beautiful woman to raise a man's spirits and speed his will to get back to bodily pleasures."

"Good heavens, the poor man has both eyes bandaged! And even if he could see, he's got other matters on his mind — like surviving. What are his chances of regaining use of his arm?"

"Ninety percent."

"And his face?"

"I'll do my best, but he may be scarred. I can see you have a lot of questions. This calls for further discussion over dinner. I have your address. I'll get you at seven — maybe a few minutes after."

Her eyes brightened with amusement. "You're amazing. You manage to turn every conversation into a proposition without even trying."

"Who said anything about a proposition? What colossal egos you girls have. I'm simply inviting you for a friendly meal. Seven o'clock?"

"Only if Ellen joins us."

"She's busy."

"So am I."

"You are not."

"Damn it, Dr. Cummings — "

"Mitch."

"I told you, Mitch — I'm not interested in being

another notch on your scoreboard. You've got a wife who I'm told adores you and half the females in the hospital drooling over you. Leave me alone. You don't need me."

"Yes, I do need you." He could feel himself swelling even as he talked to her. "I need you very much. But fortunately, I'm a patient man. When you realize how sincere I am, you'll change your mind."

Sincere about what, she wanted to ask, but stopped herself. Neither could afford to waste any more time. "When do you want to start the tubbing?"

"Five minutes," he said. "You'd better prep him."

— Chapter 16 —

"GOOD MORNING, Mr. Redington. My name's Sara. I'm a physical therapist and I'm going to do everything I can to keep you comfortable and speed your recovery."

Thus delivered of her introduction, she opened the curtains and let the morning sun stream in. The patient lay bandaged and still, but she had learned not to let sympathy impede her efficiency. "Are you having much discomfort?"

"I'm okay," he said, feeling the dressings on his head. "Are you here to give me a bath?"

"We're moving you to the treatment area. You'll be lowered on a platform into a tub of warm water. I'll explain the procedure step-by-step so you'll know exactly what to expect. You'll be well-sedated, Mr. Redington."

"If we're going to be bathing together, you'd better call me Dale."

"All right, Dale," she said, smiling. He reminded

her of her big brother Roger. "I just want you to know that it's okay to admit that it hurts, and to accept that for a short period in your life, you're going to have to be dependent."

"I don't have much choice."

"No. But you do have a choice about how you handle pain. The healthiest way is to express it — verbalize — we don't give medals for bravery."

"It's that bad?"

"It's no picnic. But we'll do everything to get the treatment done as quickly as possible." She drew a chair to his bedside. "Suppose now we try a few deep breathing exercises."

— Chapter 17 —

SARA ADJUSTED the heat shield and bent over Dale's bed. She couldn't stay long; it was like standing under a sun lamp. But neither could she leave him so soon after his ordeal.

"It's over, Dale," she whispered, patting the side of his face with a moist cloth. "The worst is over. It'll never be that bad again."

He shivered and raised a hand to reassure her. "You w-warned me," he said softly. "I was six months in the Marine Corps — Desert Storm — after Jimmy was born. I thought I'd seen every kind of human suffering. I didn't know about these tanks."

"I wish there were some painless way to remove the dead tissue, but there isn't."

"How often...?"

"We'll have to do it every day for the next few weeks. But the first debridement is by far the worst." She wiped her own forehead. "Feeling warmer?"

"A little."

"Think you can get some sleep?"

"Think so," he said, drowsily. "What's for lunch? IV tube du jour?"

"Yes, it's the house specialty." She tucked the sheet around his neck and placed the call buzzer in his hand. It hurt her to see him suffer. He seemed like such a decent, gentle man and with all the agony, he hadn't lost either his dignity or his sense of humor.

"Rest well, Dale. Just squeeze your fingers if you need me."

— Chapter 18 —
That Afternoon

SOUNDS OF A COMMOTION in the hall made Sara quicken her step towards the nursing station. "What's going on?"

"Daisy Redington arrived with enough blossoms to fill a mortuary," whispered Genelle, the day nurse. "We told her the rules and she's not happy. The resident's over there trying to calm her."

Sara turned to the noise. Immaculately coiffed and made-up, impeccable in a pink Chanel suit, Daisy Redington stood arguing with the helpless young doctor. Beside her, a hospital cart was piled high with plants and flowers.

"The whole city's been sending gifts to my husband," she was arguing. "After what he did, risking his life in that fire, why can't he enjoy being a hero?"

"I told you, Ma'am. We don't allow any fresh plants or flowers in the burn center."

"Mrs. Redington," said Sara, hurrying over. "I'm your husband's physical therapist. He's just been through a painful cleansing procedure and I'm sure he'd like you to be with him now. But if you were to bring even one rose into his room and one of the millions of bacteria on that rose were to find its way to his wound, the infection could prove fatal. That's why we're so cautious. We know you wouldn't want to jeopardize his life."

"Oh, dear! I didn't know roses were that dangerous."

"A lot of very sick people would be thrilled to have those flowers. With your permission, I could see that they're distributed to the wards."

"Yes, yes, of course. Give them to other patients."

She started to move forward, but Sara stopped her. "I'm sorry, Mrs. Redington. You'll have to put on this isolation attire before you go in. The gown opens in the back."

"They made me do this yesterday, too," she grumbled, taking the packet. "I suppose you're going to spray me with disinfectant?"

Sara smiled politely and said nothing as she helped the visitor struggle into the smock, then slide her feet into the paper slippers. "Do I have to wear this silly blue hair net?"

"Yes, please, and the gloves."

"Dale will think I'm a ghost."

"Your husband won't be too alert. He's been heavily sedated and his eyes are bandaged. Follow me, please."

Several minutes later, Daisy Redington strode out of the burn unit, and to everyone's relief, disappeared into the elevator. Sara tiptoed into Dale's room. He was either sleeping, or pretended to be, and made no sound as she straightened his covers and turned down the heat shield. The scent of Shalimar mingling with the smells of various disinfectants left a strong, unpleasant odor.

Watching the debridement, she had noticed that Dale's burns were most extensive at the elbow. She would have to start him exercising right away before scar tissue could form and limit his movement.

To the surprise of his staff, Dr. Mitchell Cummings continued to give Dale the kind of personal attention he was always too busy to give anyone else. Sara accepted her assignment conscientiously, not only because Mitch told her to, but because she tried to give every patient no less than her best. And for reasons she couldn't explain, she felt drawn to Dale. He had an inner kindness and dignity that shone through all the tubes and bandages.

The months ahead and the long, slow recovery period would be grueling, but she would do everything she could to ease his convalescence. Before he knew it, almost a year of his life would be gone — wasted on an extraordinary amount of pain and suffering. And all because he had dashed into a fire to save a man fated to die.

— Chapter 19 —

THE TALL TEENAGER smoothed his paper smock, flattened

his blue hair net self-consciously, then rapped on the door of the burn unit room and entered. A well-built redhead was bending over the bed, arranging pillows under his father's arm. "Excuse me," he said, "I'm Jim Redington. Am I disturbin' you?"

Sara turned her head with a smile. "Not at all, come in. I'm Sara, your dad's physical therapist."

What a great-looking chick, he thought, his eyes dropping to her ring finger. Damn. She wore gloves. She was probably too old for him, anyway. "Nice to meet you. I guess we can't shake hands."

"You guessed right. And you don't have to whisper. Your father's just waking up and I'm going to try to keep him up long enough to get some circulation to his toes."

"How's he doin'?"

"Dale," she said gently, "someone wants to know how you're doing."

The patient stirred and Sara motioned the young man to come closer. He grinned and moved to the bedside. "You missed a good game last night, Pop. Nicky took your seat, but he wouldn't buy me beer."

"Jimbo?" Dale raised his left hand weakly. "Why aren't you in school?"

"It's four o'clock."

"This is your third day in the hospital, Dale. You had your second skin graft this morning and it was much easier for you. Dr. Cummings is very pleased with your progress. How do you feel?"

"It — only hurts when I breathe. Jimmy — you met Sara?"

"Oh, yeah. We met. Too bad you can't see her."

"Why?"

Jimmy winked mischievously. "Well, she's very nice-lookin' for a woman her age. No disrespect, Ma'am, but you're about fifty?"

Sara winked back. "You flatter me, young man."

"She looks a little like Nana, Dad. Short, gray hair — very neat, of course. And those glasses, sort of like Nana wears. Same height, only kinda heavier — no offense, Ma'am."

"Jimmy!"

"It's all right, Dale. I'm fat and frumpy and don't mind a bit. The pretty young nurses have to fight off doctors all day. Thank God they leave me alone."

Jimmy cupped his mouth to control the giggles.

"Could you — turn on the heat shield?" asked Dale.

"It's already on. It'll warm up in a few seconds. I'd like to massage your legs, but I'll come back later if you want to be alone with your son."

"He's — seen my legs." An involuntary groan escaped as Dale tried to move.

"I know it hurts." Sara rolled back the covers and pulled down his gown. "I have some good news. Your kidneys are producing urine by the gallon. That's an excellent sign. We've cut down your fluid intake."

"My eyes?"

"Dr. Schwartz will be in this evening. He'll tell you when the blinders come off."

"Everythin's fine at home, Dad," said Jimmy, trying to sound cheerful. "People keep callin' an askin' about you.

Mom's gonna be on some radio show talkin' about opera, but she says she's sure the guy's gonna ask about you. I'll be at school, but I could get Nana to tape it."

"Don't both'r."

"Okay. Mom wanted me to go to the opera with her last night, but I told her no way. She took her hairdresser, you know, Kenni with an 'i'? He told Mom she looked gorgeous but he kept starin' at me. He invited me to visit his art studio. I said I'd go if I could bring my girlfriend —" He glanced over at Sara. "I don't even have a girlfriend. Hey, am I talkin' too much?"

"Not at all," she said, continuing to knead Dale's calf. "It's the first time I've seen your father smile."

Jimmy rattled on another ten minutes and Dale answered in brief sentences, obviously enjoying the visit. The boy left when Mitch stopped by to examine his patient. The surgeon seemed pleased and announced that Dale was making excellent progress.

— **Chapter 20** —

SHORTLY AFTER MITCH LEFT, the psychiatrist, Dr. Tatsuko Hoshido, poked his head in the door to Dale's room and asked Sara to join him at the nursing station.

"You seem to be spending an unusual amount of time with this patient," he noted, leafing through the file.

"Mitch knows the family," she answered. "He ordered special treatment."

The doctor peered over his glasses. "I hope the other patients aren't getting shortchanged."

"I see them, too, although I suspect I was hired mainly to attend to Mr. Redington. He sleeps a lot, almost never complains and he's very quiet. If I were in his place, I wouldn't feel like making chit-chat either."

"Who visits him?"

"Family. His wife flits in and out. We all breathe a sigh of relief when she leaves. I think Dale does, too. But he perks up when his parents or his fourteen-year-old son come by. Outside of that, he won't see or talk to anyone."

"No friends?"

"They phone sometime. I answer and say he's not taking calls. Someone named Bernie, I think — says she's his old nanny — keeps calling to ask how he's doing."

"No other problems?" he asked, scribbling on a clipboard.

"Not that I've noticed, Dr. Hoshido. How does he seem to you?"

"Withdrawn. Depressed. Normal anxiety reactions to severe bodily trauma. He's still adjusting. He could have complications when the reality hits him."

"But he'll recover?"

"If all goes well. He's facing heavy surgery, the strain of learning to live with scars and possible disfigurement. Constant pain for months. The transition back to normal life."

"I'll watch for any signs of depression. Now if you'll excuse me, I'd better look in on him."

"All right. But Sara — don't get too involved."

"Involved?" She spun around in surprise. "What makes you say that?"

"You can't help it — spending so much time with a patient. I just hope you have a husband or a partner you care about at home. Someone you can talk to. It's important to keep a balance."

For a moment, she wondered why he was curious about her love life, then she realized that Mitch was making her paranoid, making her think that every man who made a personal comment had ulterior motives — even poor Doc Hoshido, almost sixty, well-respected in the hospital and known for boring everyone with pictures of his grandkids. He was no more interested in seducing her than he was in running for President.

"Don't worry," she said, smiling. "I'm not the least bit involved with my patient — and I don't intend to be."

— **Chapter 21** —

LYING FLAT ON HIS BACK unable to see was grim, tedious and boring — more boring than any board of directors' meeting, more boring than those interminable flights to Paris, drearier than the endless social events Daisy dragged him to — or used to drag him to.

Dale groped on the nightstand for his water. Now that the feeding tube was out, he could take liquids through a straw. His family could visit without wearing isolation gowns. He had even been able to eat cream of broccoli soup at lunch — and he hated broccoli.

The cool water slid down his throat and he replaced the glass on the table. Thank God his insides were intact, or so everyone told him. Would he ever function as a normal human being again? What would life be like once he got home? Nothing would be the same, that was certain. The robust good health he'd always taken for granted had become a commodity — one he'd almost lost and one he would spend many months fighting to regain.

But he would regain it. His will to survive was strong, and fortunately he was in the hands of experts. To his amazement, people like Mitch and Sara, even the residents and nurses, seemed to care about him. It was strange to know their voices, yet not know the first thing about them.

Considering his son's penchant for practical jokes, the description of Sara as a hefty over-50-year-old was suspect, yet she herself had confirmed the description. Not that it mattered. She was a lovely woman who treated him with tenderness and concern, and he would always be grateful to her for getting him through one of the worst weeks of his life.

The months to come, he realized, were not going to be easy. Everyone, including the psychiatrist, had warned him of rough times ahead. Well, so be it. Maybe this whole incident had happened for the best. Maybe he'd needed a jolt to shake him out of his rut.

In retrospect, it all seemed clear. How could he have tolerated that life for fifteen years? He worked at the paper company because his father wanted him to, and because going into the family business had been a *fait accompli* since birth. But was it what he wanted to do?

And the other. Flying to Europe to attend parties and openings, vacationing in Palm Beach and on the

French Riviera, running with the international set, had all been to keep Daisy happy — it was what she wanted.

The constant pressures of job and socializing, however, had left time for little else. How he missed seeing some of his old Marine buddies, going fishing with the guys, getting involved with causes, even plunking out tunes on the piano.

"It's ten to five, Dale." Sara's soft words broke into his reverie. Her voice pleased him. From what he could sense, she was a solid, no-nonsense woman who seemed at ease with men and played no games.

"I talked to the psychiatrist you saw earlier today," she continued. "He says you appear to be mentally sound, which is more than I can say about most people — including myself."

Dale managed a half-smile. "Going home?"

"Yes. I freshened your water and turned your radio to the classical music station. By the way, a woman — Bernie something — keeps calling and leaving her number. I, uh — haven't mentioned it to anyone. I'll call her back if you'd like."

"Oh, that's Birdy — my old nanny. Yes, please call, tell her that we'll solve her problem when I get home. Would you also call my accountant, Eddie Powell? He's in the phone book and works late. Tell him to raise Birdy's pension $400 a month. And Sara, could all this be confidential?"

"Yes, of course. I'll call as soon as I get home. Now please try to relax. Dagmar's here if you need anything. Care for a sleeping pill?"

"No, thanks. Too many pills."

"Happy dreams, then, and I'll see you tomorrow."

The door closed with a squeak, leaving Dale alone and lonely, dreading the long night ahead.

— Chapter 22 —

AN HOUR LATER, back in her own kitchen, Sara looked up Mr. Powell's number, then called. He asked a few questions to confirm her identity and finally agreed to honor Dale's request.

Next call was to Birdy, and Sara couldn't help wondering if this doting woman could secretly be Dale's mistress. Although he didn't seem like the philandering type, he *was* male, after all, and it was obvious to everyone that he was not enamored with Daisy.

A few minutes into the call, however, dispelled all doubts. Birdy's mature, raspy voice and her tearful reaction to the report of Dale's suffering, convinced Sara that this was no floozy girlfriend, but indeed, an ex-nanny who truly cared about him.

The fact that Dale had asked Sara to call her, told Birdy that Dale trusted her. Realizing she could finally talk to someone, Birdy's words gushed out, as she related Dale's visit to her home the day of the fire and the troubling situation with baby Vicky. Birdy's need to talk seemed almost frantic; up to that moment, she had confided in no one but Dale. Now, at last, this kind woman would put her back in touch with him.

— Chapter 23 —

EARLY THE NEXT MORNING, Dale's temperature zoomed to 105. The hospitalist on duty discovered his intestinal tract was not functioning. Nurses re-inserted the feeding tube and began pumping him full of antibiotics. Feverish, disoriented, full of medication and unable to see or understand what was happening, Dale began to hallucinate.

Dr. Hoshido answered the emergency call and spent half an hour with his patient. He changed the medication, explained that the physical and emotional stresses had caused a temporary brain imbalance, and tried to teach Dale how to separate delusions from reality. By the time the doctor left, the visions had stopped.

Sara was quietly closing Dale's door when his mother came hurrying toward her. "Bad time for a visit?"

"I'm afraid so, Mrs. Redington. Dale loves to see you, but he had some complications this morning and he needs his sleep."

"Serious?"

"Nothing unexpected. He'll be better tomorrow."

"I wish you'd call me 'Fran.' Could you squeeze in a cup of coffee?"

"Gosh, I don't — wait a minute. Sure, I can. I forgot to have lunch today!"

Minutes later, the two women faced each other across a small, square table in the hospital cafeteria. Sara spread a napkin on her lap, bit into her tuna sandwich and seemed to see her companion for the first time.

Until that moment, Frances Redington had simply been "Dale's mother" — short of stature, but A-plus in grace and presence. She bore little resemblance to her son, at least to the tall, handsome man in the newspaper picture taken before the fire. The only similarity was their coloring.

Both had brownish-black hair, but Fran's was too black to be natural. It framed a once-pretty oval face, now stamped with a permanent worried expression. Yet her daily visits always seemed to calm her son.

"A penny?" asked Fran, emptying a Splenda envelope into her coffee.

Sara laughed. "Sorry. I guess I was thinking what a remarkable woman you are and what a wonderful bond you have with Dale."

"Walter and I are blessed with our son. And I've been wanting to tell you what a blessing you are, too. Your care, your gentleness, your professionalism — they mean a lot to Dale."

"He's a strong, brave man. I shouldn't say this, but somehow, I don't see him as the jet-setting 'socialite' in the newspaper article."

"He's anything but. And I hate that word! It reminds me of some of the frozen-faced gals at our 'Symphony Saviors' meetings. They squeeze 'volunteer' work in between their hair and their Botox appointments, don't know Brahms from Bartok and couldn't care less about the Symphony. Of course, they're all friends of Daisy's. But that's another story."

"I've noticed that your daughter-in-law can be — a bit scattered?"

"You're very diplomatic. But I need you to tell me what's happening with Dale. Mitch said he was hallucinating, but that it's not serious. The truth, please?"

Sara lifted her sandwich, then set it down again. For the moment, food was secondary. "Mitch told you the truth. It's not uncommon for patients with severe burns to have delusions. In Dale's case, being sightless made it worse. But Dr. Hoshido, the psychiatrist, wants to keep the eye patches in place till Dale is calm and lucid and can handle the transition."

"He's lucid now, isn't he?"

"He's almost back to normal. Dr. Schwartz — the ophthalmologist — agreed to wait a few days, then remove the eye patches Friday morning. Daisy said she'll be here."

"What good can *she* do? What if there's a problem and Dale can't see?"

"There's little chance of that. Both eyes had only slight corneal damage."

"Oh, my poor boy!" Fran took a last sip of coffee. "Mind if I ask your age?"

"Twenty-seven."

"Married?"

"No." Sara smiled. "I came close, but escaped in time."

"Well, some lucky man will snap you up soon. Thanks for the chat and please forgive me if I spoke too frankly. I'll see you tomorrow, and at nine on Friday."

"You're coming, too?"

"Just like Daisy, my dear. I can't stand to miss an opening."

— Chapter 24 —

DALE LAY ON HIS BACK, his head propped on a pillow, his brain seething with anger. Why did everything have to be a production?

Gathering the clan for the removal of his blinders had to be Daisy's idea. If there were some way she could make a non-event into a social occasion, she would do it, then plead innocence when it appeared in the newspaper.

"But Dale, I haven't talked to Leah in weeks! I can't imagine who gave her that item." It used to amaze him that she could look him in the eye and lie without blinking a lash.

"How's our patient this morning?"

The voice was professional, with a touch of concern. Dale held his temper. "I'm okay, Dr. Schwartz. Who else is out there?"

"Your parents, your wife, your son, Hadley Harris and of course, Mitch."

"No photographers? No friends?"

"Your mother shooed them away."

"Thank God!"

At that moment, the door opened. Daisy entered, followed by the others. "Hi, honeybun, how do you feel?"

He froze as she kissed his forehead. "Fine. Let's get this over with."

The eye doctor slid on his gloves. "Nothing to worry about, Dale. This won't hurt. Just keep your eyes closed till I tell you to open them."

Bending over his patient, he gently loosened the

tape, then carefully lifted the patches and set them on a tray that Sara was holding. "Now stay shut, please. It looks good — no sign of infection. I'm just going to clean you up a bit."

A moment later, the doctor motioned to Mitch to turn down the blinds. "Your vision may be fuzzy at first while the residues of medication wash away. Now — let's give it a try."

The room was silent with anticipation as Dale blinked several times, conditioned himself to the light, then opened his eyes wide and stared straight ahead. "Yes..." he said softly, "Yes, I can see!" His body trembled with relief as he raised his left hand and made a small two-fingered circle.

Applause broke the heavy silence. Tears flowed down Fran Redington's cheek, Walter and the doctors grinned, Sara raised a triumphant fist and Mitch cried, "Bravo!"

One of several blurred figures around the bed waved at him. The glitter of a diamond told him whose hand it was.

"I can see you, Daisy," he said excitedly. The visitors were coming into focus.

"Can you see me, Dad?"

"Sure, I can see you, Jimbo. Dr. Schwartz, could you please put back the blinders?"

"Very funny, Dad. Can you really see me?"

"Yes. Get a haircut."

"You appear to be completely healed!" The physician examined Dale's pupils with a beam of light. "Open the blinds a bit more — that's good. Now, can you see across the room?"

"Yes, it's almost in focus. Hi, Mom, Dad, Hadley, Mitch...and?" He stopped and caught his breath. A most extraordinary-looking woman stood by the window. Rays of sunlight bounced off her fiery red hair, large blue eyes twinkled with kindness and she was smiling at him.

"I'm — sorry," he said, "I don't think I know you."

"Well, I know you, Dale." Sara walked over to his bed, pulled up the covers and tucked them around his shoulders. "You mustn't get chilled. I'm turning on the heat shield for a few minutes while you visit with your family."

"I'll be damned," he whispered. "You're frumpy Sara?"

Before she could answer, Daisy pulled up a chair and sat herself down. "You can go now, Sara," she said, waving a dismissive hand. "We'll buzz if we need you."

"Wait a minute — don't go! May I have a mirror?"

"Let her go, honeybun, she has to earn her wages." Daisy fumbled in her purse while Sara and Mitch disappeared out the door. "I have a compact — here, have a look."

Dale took the mirror and stared. The sight of his pale, bandaged face, blistered skin and misshapen smile made him recoil. "Holy shit," he muttered. "No wonder you kept me blind."

Fran Redington moved to the bed, snatched the compact and handed it back to Daisy with a frown. "It's only been eleven days since the fire, dear. You can't expect to heal overnight."

"No one told me I look like Frankenstein's monster."

"Mitch is the best reconstructive surgeon there is. He's promised he can fix you up almost as good as new — maybe better."

"Thanks, Mom. I — I'm tired. If you all don't mind, I'd like to get some rest."

Daisy patted his covers. "I'll stay with you."

"No, please. Take Jimbo and go home."

"He's right," said Dr. Schwartz, moving to the door and holding it open. "It's time for everyone to leave, including me."

— Chapter 25 —

THE MINUTE he was alone, Dale pressed his buzzer — twice. One squeeze would bring the nurse, two for Sara. No wonder his son had teased about her looks. What a surprise! What a knockout! What an incredible beauty!

Perhaps it was just as well he hadn't seen her before. The idea of the nurses wiping his bottom didn't faze him in the least, but the image of that exquisite creature massaging his groin or repositioning his catheter and complimenting him on his urine flow, made him flush with embarrassment. What if he were to get an erection? Little chance of that in his miserable state, he thought. He'd be lucky if he ever got one again.

Responding to his call, Sara appeared, pleasant and professional, as always. Little had changed for her, he realized, but everything had changed for him. Her remark about pretty young nurses having to fight off doctors came back to him; she must have been talking about herself.

"Warm enough?" she asked, turning off the heat shield. "I know it was a nuisance having all those people around, but they wanted to share your happiness."

"I'm sorry Daisy was rude."

"Don't give it a thought. I used to fight with my brothers a lot, then I learned that getting upset wasn't worth the headaches I got. So I grew thick skin and just let their remarks slide off me."

"You have brothers?"

Sara laughed. "Does the Pope pray? I've got them in all sizes. If anyone tried to bully me, I'd say, 'I'll get my brothers after you!' When they found out I meant it, they left me alone. Roger's the oldest. Once I walked up behind him when he was swinging a baseball bat and I got a huge lump on my head plus a black eye. But now we're best friends. I love the other two, but Roger's my soul mate."

Hearing Sara talk about herself for the first time delighted Dale. Maybe she was trying to distract him from his pain and his problems. More likely, he'd been too self-involved to show much interest in anyone else. He noticed she wore no wedding ring. "Do you live with your family?"

"I share an apartment with a girlfriend. My family's in Seattle. My dad named me after some woman architect who built buildings — he loves that city. Dad and my middle brother Andrew are pediatricians there, and my baby brother Gary's in law school. By the way, Birdy sends you love, said to tell you Vicky's fine and your accountant will honor your request."

"Thanks for taking care of all that. Birdy told you about Vicky?"

"Yes, she seemed to have a need to tell me the whole sad story — in strictest confidence. Don't worry, my brothers always confided in me. My parents would expire on the spot if they knew what I know. Anyway, Dr. Hoshido wants you to practice your visualization, so suppose you start thinking about getting well while I exercise your legs."

Dale lay back, closed his eyes, and for the moment, let his mind stray where it would. He had survived eleven days of sightlessness, two skin graft surgeries, a bout of insanity and the daily tank baths he called "torture therapy." The physical struggle was far from over, but he no longer had any doubts of the outcome. With the help of one of the kindest, most beautiful women he had ever seen, his future was looking brighter by the minute.

— Chapter 26 —
2008 — 2009

"WE'VE GOT TO MAKE a decision about Dale Redington."

Sara, Dr. Tatsuko Hoshido, Dr. Hadley Harris, several residents and nurses, sat around the conference table, their eyes fixed on the director. Attendance at the weekly burn team meeting was mandatory, and the only time the staff got together to compare notes about the patients.

"Dale starts his seventh week here tomorrow," Mitch Cummings explained. "I've finished the major autografts and the rest can be done on an outpatient basis. You may have noticed he's been getting out of his wheelchair lately and starting to walk. How's he doing, Sara?"

"It's very painful, but he tries to take a few steps every hour. The main problem is that we've been replacing his oxycodone with suboxone, yet he's still having bad symptoms. And he shouldn't be having any."

"What kind of symptoms?" asked a resident.

"Chills, cramps, pains, edgy nerves, vomiting, diarrhea. As I mentioned to you before, Mitch, I don't know who's screwing up, but I'd be willing to bet Dale's still getting some kind of opiate."

"Calm down, Sara. No one screwed up. Every patient reacts differently."

"But she's right, Mitch, Dale should *not* be having symptoms." Hadley Harris frowned and looked toward the residents. "We have a record of not getting our patients addicted to medication. We've had an occasional problem with oxycodone, which, as you know, is an opioid, like morphine. But we've never had a full-blown addiction withdrawal."

He paused to let his words register. "Suboxone, or Bupenorphine, is a partial opiate and a wonderful drug that allows patients to withdraw from painkillers gently. It's expensive and it could take several months, but it works. Dale should *not* be suffering withdrawal. After the meeting, Sara, let's review the dosage. Dale can continue using the Suboxone on an outpatient basis."

"You mean he can go home?" she asked.

Mitch looked to the psychiatrist. "What say you, Tatsuko?"

"The patient may need further psychotherapy. But

as far as going home, yes, it's a good idea."

"Hadley?" asked Mitch.

"Pack him up and send him back to Daisy."

Laughter rippled through the room.

"Everyone agree he's ready to be cut loose?" Heads nodded as Mitch continued, "All right. I'm doing more facial surgery Monday. If all goes well and there's no reason it shouldn't, I'll set his discharge date for two weeks from today, Friday, January 23rd. No, make it the 24th. That way, we'll have two more sessions to evaluate him. In the meantime, Sara, talk to Daisy, set up regular home visits from the nurses and arrange for him to come in at least once a week for PT. Now, about that pesky Mrs. Wilson…"

— Chapter 27 —

LATER THAT DAY, Sara knocked lightly and entered Mitch's office. "You wanted to see me?"

"Yes. Close the door. Have a seat."

She took a chair opposite the desk and waited for him to stop writing. He looked up and smiled. "You're even more enticing than usual today. New hairdo?"

"No, same old hairdo." And same old line of bullshit, she thought. Would he ever get the message?

"I'm glad we have this chance to talk — alone. We're going to have to make our big move soon, while Dale's still in our clutches. My gut feeling is that we ought to strike now. He's mentioned several times how grateful he is — I'd like to get a commitment for our clinic while he's in a generous mood — what do you think?"

"It's not our clinic, Mitch, it's yours. And I want nothing to do with asking him for money."

"What do you mean?" The surgeon's voice rose with irritation. "I thought we were in this together. Aren't you planning to come with me and be my administrative assistant?"

"I didn't know you'd made me an offer." She hesitated, not wanting to promise anything, yet not sure she wanted to turn him down. "How much money will it take to build your clinic?"

"Twenty million up front. I've no interest in setting up a second-rate operation. Everything has to be the newest and best, the very latest in equipment and technology. If I could get the Frances and Walter Redington Foundation to donate the initial funds, I have friends who'll come in as investors."

"Then why not talk to the senior Redingtons? Why bother Dale?"

"Because, my beauty, mommy and daddy will do anything their beloved son wants. By the way, I see you've been getting chummy with Frances."

Sara stiffened, instantly alert. "We've had coffee a few times. I like her."

"Perfect! Be as friendly with her as you can."

"Now look, Mitch — "

"It won't hurt you. You could even start being nice to Daisy. We're going to need her on our side."

"I'm always polite to that airhead."

He sighed. "Daisy Redington is our entrée to high society. She's already invited Ellen and me to a dinner party next week. I intend to be so witty and charming and to flatter the ladies so outrageously, they'll all be breaking their rich bottoms to invite us to their next soirée."

"That's what you want?"

"It's what we want, don't you see? These are the women who'll be our patrons — our clients. The more I can squeeze into their snotty little cliques, the more I can earn their trust and friendship and the more likely they are to come to me when they need a lift — both mental and physical."

"Sounds like a waste of time and effort. Your work and your reputation are what will bring clients."

"It's no waste, I promise you. These ladies never want to grow old. They're determined to slink into their sixties and seventies in sequined gowns, and they're going to need our help to do it. They'll pay almost anything to prolong their youth, and if we don't tighten their flab and tuck their faces, someone else will. I've been trying to break into this market for a long time, Sara, and I'm not going to let anything fuck up the opportunity. Especially not you."

Her expression was impassive as she stood up. "Is that all?"

"I'm warning you and I'm deadly serious. I've told Genelle, Dagmar and the rest of my staff, too. You girls had better start playing kissy-ass with Daisy, or you'll find yourself out in the cold."

"May I go now?"

"Yes. But first tell me — you know Dale better than anyone. Do you think he'd be more receptive to a request

81

before I start the extensive reconstruction of his face?"

"No, I'd wait. He's dealing with a lot of anxiety now, and if you do a great job, which you will, he'll be relieved and grateful."

Before he could comment, Sara turned and strode out of the office.

— Chapter 28 —

AFTER A WEEKEND of stomach spasms and pains, Dale seemed to have weathered the worst of his withdrawal and fell into a deep slumber. He awoke to find Sara standing by his bed.

" 'Morning, sleeping beauty," she said, holding up a small rubber ball. "Squeeze this with your right hand when you're more awake. How do you feel?"

"Like a Mack truck ran over my chest." Dale tried to sit up, then lay down again.

"Please — take it easy." She raised his head gently and smoothed his forehead. "It's odd — you took the suboxone, yet you still had withdrawal symptoms. Dr. Harris checked the dosage and you shouldn't have suffered. Has anyone been fussing with your IV?"

"Only the staff. You think someone was giving me drugs I didn't need?"

"Yes, Dale, just between us, I'm certain of it. You should've been well enough to go home a week ago. But whoever goofed, that IV is gone and you'll be going home soon, so you can take your daily suboxone yourself. Speaking of same, lift your tongue, please."

Dale smiled and complied; Sara placed a tablet in his mouth. "Don't chew or swallow, let it melt," she reminded him. "I'll be back in ten minutes."

"I can't imagine that anyone who went through the hell of oxycodone withdrawal, would even think of going back on drugs," Dale murmured as Sara returned to check his pulse. He started to groan, then stopped himself. She mustn't think him a complainer. "You've spoiled me, you know. I've got to learn to be self-sufficient. What day is it?"

"Monday. January twelfth. I was off this weekend, but you didn't miss me. I'm told that you slept much of the time."

"Of course I missed you. When do I go home?"

"Saturday, the twenty-fourth. Less than two weeks away. Looking forward?"

"Yes and no." Daisy had told him she'd moved him out of their bedroom into the guest room. He'd be glad for his privacy, but he'd also have to endure whatever strange nurses or attendants she would hire to look after him.

And he would miss Sara — terribly. He would miss her care…her voice…her smile…the ringlets of red hair poking out of her plastic cap…the outline of her full breasts under the blue, tight-waisted uniform…the touch of her hands on his body… "Any chance of your coming home with me?"

Sara laughed. "Don't think you're getting rid of me just because you're leaving. Mitch wants you to come in for physical therapy at least once a week."

"Good! I don't want anyone but you to torture me."

She straightened his head on the pillow. "I'm afraid it's Mitch's turn this morning. I'm sorry."

"Oh, no. More surgery?"

Sara nodded. "That's why you haven't had breakfast. They'll be getting you in about half an hour."

A wave of despair swept over him. Would it never end? The minute he started to feel human again, they would shoot him full of sedatives and wheel him off to the OR.

"Damn it, Sara, I don't want to have my face worked on. I don't care what I look like and I sure as hell don't need any more drugs pumped into me. Can't we cancel the damn operation?"

She stopped exercising his arm and began rubbing the back of his neck. "Dale — try to relax. It's reconstructive surgery. The skin on your face won't heal by itself. It has to be grafted."

He sighed aloud, closed his eyes and tried to think about the light lemony scent wafting up to him as she bent over his chest. Another twelve days and he would be home. No one could force him to have more operations, no one would wake him at midnight to give him a sleeping pill, and no one could turn him into a medical junkie — ever again.

PART 4

— Chapter 29 —

January, 2009

DESPITE HIS WISHES, Dale's next twelve days were crammed full of surgical procedures, instructions on changing dressings, fittings for the elastic pressure garments he would have to wear to decrease scar formation, advice on diet and nutrition, psychiatric counseling and the many preparations needed for his release from the burn unit.

The social worker invited his family to a support group meeting; all but Daisy attended. Frances Redington later told Sara that the session was "of dubious value."

The day of his discharge, nurse Genelle helped Dale dress in loose-fitting sweats, while Sara brought in the wheelchair. Daisy and Mitch arrived together, chatting, laughing and flirting so blatantly that Sara felt embarrassed for Dale.

She started to wheel him down the hall, but Mitch grabbed her arm. "I'll take it from here," he insisted. "My favorite patient deserves a personal escort."

And off they went, Dale giving Sara a weak wave, knowing better than to show affection in front of his wife — although, from all appearances, Daisy and Mitch were intimately involved, or else working up to it. Still, he couldn't let himself believe that Mitch, his good friend and highly attentive physician, would be sleeping with his wife. Not that Daisy wouldn't be willing.

Driving home in the black limo she'd pestered him to buy for them, Dale's thoughts raced back to the time, about five years into their marriage, when he first learned of her infidelity. A college fraternity brother felt he owed it to his old pal to report he'd seen Daisy and a young man kissing passionately in a dark restaurant, south of Market

Street. She'd come home late that night with tales of a car accident.

His own reaction, Dale recalled, had not been anger so much as hurt and disappointment. Her occasional dalliances had continued; he'd hear snippets of phone calls, observe her hastily cover up her emails when he passed her computer, see her return from "Symphony meetings" with red cheeks and mussed hair. He knew all the signs, he'd just been too busy to do anything about them. That, he promised himself, would change.

Early that evening, Daisy gave her husband a quick peck on the forehead, then went off to "a movie with the girls." The thought crossed Dale's mind that she might be meeting Mitch, but he put that thought aside. Sara had told him that Mitch loved the ladies, but the man had integrity — of that he was sure.

He was not sorry to see Daisy leave, however, and promptly sent his nurse to the drug store for bandages he didn't need, made sure the household staff was not within hearing distance, then grabbed the phone and called his former nanny.

"Birdy, it's Dale — home at last!"

"Oh, thank Heavens! How do you feel? The hospital would never let me talk to you. So glad you had your physical therapist call me."

"All's well and I'm thrilled to be home. How are you? How's Vicky?"

"She gets cuter and sweeter all the time. I don't suppose I can bring her over to see you."

"I'm afraid not. But if you ever need me, you can call Sara — Sara Bowman at St. Paul's Hospital. She's the woman you talked to. Are you okay financially?"

"Yes, thanks to your monthly checks — and the generous increase."

"Babies cost money. I remember, I was one, once. And the missing mother?"

"Not a peep. Jenna and Shane had been renting the house, so the owner took charge but he hasn't cleaned it up or put it on the market yet."

"Did anyone ask questions?"

"The owners asked if I knew where Jenna was, and of course I didn't and don't."

Dale shook his head. "Curiouser and curiouser. I had lots of time to think when I was lying there in the hospital. You mentioned Jenna had a midwife when she gave birth. Were you there?"

"No, Jenna hired this 'homebirth practitioner' she found online. She called to tell me when she was starting labor. Her contractions were five minutes apart. I saw the midwife arrive twenty minutes later, lugging a suitcase."

"How long was she there?"

"About three hours. Jenna said she gave birth normally, without anesthetic. Then the woman clamped and cut the umbilical cord, and sutured her lacerations with lidocaine to numb the pain. I stayed all week to help Jenna and the baby."

"Didn't the midwife have to report to someone?"

"Yes, Vicky has a birth certificate — she's legal."

"Can you keep caring for her until I get there? It

may be months before I can drive."

"That's fine. Vicky's thriving. You'll be amazed how she's grown."

"Well, don't confide in anyone, Birdy. Not a soul. Just keep thinking of any friends of Jenna's you might have met, anything she might have said to explain why she felt vulnerable and why she didn't want anyone to know about Vicky. Sooner or later, we'll get some answers."

— Chapter 30 —

ALONE IN HER KITCHEN that evening, Sara found herself staring at the newspaper, unable to concentrate. At the hospital, nurse Genelle, who'd accompanied Dale, Daisy and Mitch to the exit, had reported: "Dale seemed glad to be going home and Daisy pretended to be glad, but couldn't take her eyes off Mitch. He helped me get Dale into the car and the couple sped off to their love nest."

A wave of sadness came over Sara. Daisy would have hired round-the-clock caregivers. The thought of that gentle, courageous man being cared for by strangers was disturbing.

Strolling into the kitchen, she made herself a cup of instant cocoa, added a marshmallow, then returned to the table. The front page of the newspaper danced in her head, a jumble of words and phrases that held no meaning as she tried vainly to concentrate. Finally, with a sigh, she reached for the phone.

"Is Roger there?" she asked the woman who answered.

"May I say who it is?"

"His sister in San Francisco."

The tone was suddenly friendly. "Oh, hello. I'm Natasha. I'll get him for you."

A patter of quick footsteps, then Roger's booming voice. "Why didn't you call me Sunday?"

He was getting almost as possessive as their father. "I told you I might go to a movie, remember? Oh, Roger, Dale went home today and I really feel crummy — as if I've deserted him."

"Do you feel that way about all your patients?"

"Of course not. But Dale's been on my mind almost constantly for the last eight weeks. Suddenly he's gone and there's this great void —"

"Are you in love with him?"

"No, no, I just feel guilty turning him over to that dizzy wife and a bunch of private nurses who won't know how to care for him. Mitch told him not to touch his bandages, but he's going to want to look at his face pretty soon and he's going to be depressed. Mitch doesn't know if he can ever erase the scars."

"It's not your problem, Sis. You did all you could for him. You've got to let go."

"I've sure tried." Talking to her brother was an instant catharsis. She felt better already. "Tell me about you. Who's Natasha? Is she right there?"

"Very much so."

"Anything serious? Yes or no."

"Good question. Shall we observe our usual Sunday night ritual?"

"Gotcha. I'll call tomorrow. I wonder who'll answer. Will it be Natasha or someone else?"

"Neither. Even God had to rest on the seventh day."

"Okay," she said, laughing. Her spirits lifted, Sara gave up on the newspaper, soaked in a hot bubble bath and crawled into bed with a copy of David Baldacci's latest thriller. If anyone could get her mind off of Dale, Mr. B. could do it.

— Chapter 31 —

LATE THE NEXT AFTERNOON, Sara was surprised by Roger's voice on the phone. "I couldn't wait for your call," he explained. "I have good news."

"Natasha's pregnant and I'm invited to the wedding?"

"Bite your tongue," he growled. "Natasha's right here with me and I told her about Dale. She says her sister was badly burned in her kitchen last year and the doctors said she'd always be scarred. But she went to this medical clinic place in Wisconsin — apparently it specializes in burn reconstruction — and today, you can't tell she ever had an accident."

"Really?" Sara resisted the urge to remind him this was his day of rest. "Put Natasha on, please?"

"Hi, Sis," said a warm voice. "You want the name of the medical clinic?"

"I'd love to hear more about it. Who runs it?"

"Dr. Cossa — first name Antonio. He's from Brazil, well-known there and apparently has quite a following.

People from all over the world fly in just to see him. Actually, it's much more than a medical clinic, more like a fancy spa. And horribly expensive, as I recall."

"Did your sister have bad scars?"

"Very bad. Dr. Cossa's surgery is traditional and mainstream, but he also keeps up on what's new medically. The clinic staff is more into herbs and supplements and alternative therapies. All I know is that he performed a miracle on my sister."

Sara grabbed a pencil. "C-O-S-S-A?"

"Yes, but Google E-L-I-V-A, pronounced el-EE-va. That's the name of the clinic; it's near Appleton, Wisconsin. You can download the brochure. They have a video, too. They mainly do burn reconstruction."

"Thanks so much, Natasha, I'll get right on it. Give my big brother a hug."

'With pleasure," she said.

Before Sara could reach her computer, heels clacked in the hallway.

"It's your long lost housemate," called Hallie, "home for some warm clothes. Cas and I are going skiing tomorrow — back next Monday."

"Taking the week off? What fun!" Sara greeted her landlady with a hug and the offer of hot cocoa. "Can you sit down for three minutes? I'm dying to ask you something."

"Shoot," said Hallie, dropping into a chair. As friends and family all knew, she didn't care to waste words or time. Patience, she would readily admit, was not among her assets.

"Okay. If you're so in love with Mr. Fantastic, why aren't you living together?"

"Glad you asked. I told you Cas and I met on a luxury cruise ship. When we came home and told my Mom we were getting married, she had a fit. Said we'd only known each other a few weeks and in very romantic circumstances which had nothing to do with reality."

"Smart woman."

"Mom's a control freak like you wouldn't believe, but she's no dummy. She begged us to wait two years, *not* living together so I could date others — big joke. If we still want to get married by Christmas of 2010, she'll host the wedding and buy us a house."

"And if you don't wait?"

"We didn't even consider that. Cas said right away to take her offer — that he could never afford to buy the kind of home I'd want and he's right. I'm totally spoiled. So we accepted her conditions and I rented this apartment. I live here, but no one said I have to sleep here."

Sara laughed. "Good for you and good for Cas for being practical. One more question?"

Hallie glanced at her watch. "Sure."

Stressing the need for confidence, Sara related Birdy's story about baby Vicky and how her mother, Jenna Snow, had disappeared. "Dale's determined to find out what happened to Jenna," she explained, "but he's not healed enough to do the legwork. I'd like to help but I don't know where to start. Any ideas?"

"Would that be Jenna Snow from the Golden Gate Star?"

"I think so. She did work at a local newspaper."

"We used to email when I was pitching story ideas for clients. She was always pleasant. Then all of a sudden she was gone and there was a new associate editor. I'll talk to Cas — he'll have some ideas."

"I hate to bother him."

"And I hate to brag, but he's a prize-winning investigative journalist. He loves stuff like that — nothing better than a good mystery. And a good story, of course."

"But he can't write about it. If anyone finds out, the authorities will take baby Vicky and put her in the system. Besides, Jenna could still be alive."

Hallie stood up. "How 'bout if Cas calls and talks to Dale next week when we get back?"

"Fabulous — thanks. But tell Cas, please, not a word to anyone. And maybe have him call Dale around eleven a.m., when his wife's not there."

"Oh?"

Sara blushed. "It's not what you're thinking. We're just friends."

"Sure, you are." Hallie grinned and handed her a scratch pad. "Write down his number, please."

— **Chapter 32** —
Eight Days Later
February, 2009

THE GRAY STONE MANSION on Broadway Street, the so-called "Gold Coast" of San Francisco, was unusually quiet Monday morning, Dale's tenth day at home.

Daisy had gone off to her bridge lesson, Jimmy was at school, the maid and the butler were downstairs minding their business and he'd just fired his nurse.

The young woman had refused to leave at first, but Dale paid her extra and assured her that he was quite able to care for himself until tomorrow, when he'd be seeing the doctor.

As soon as she closed the door, Dale called the agency and canceled the nurses Daisy had ordered for the rest of the week. What a relief not to have those bossy females hovering over him!

To his surprise and gratification, his left hand had become adept at minor chores, he'd been able to trade his walker for a cane, and he felt himself getting more self-reliant every day.

Besides, he was finally going to see Sara in the physical therapy center tomorrow, right after he saw Mitch. She would help him out of his pressure garments, sponge his chest and run him through his exercises. As long as he still had her to look after him, he didn't need — or want — anyone else.

What a lucky break it had been, he thought, smiling to himself, to have had her incredible care and professionalism from the first day of his ordeal. What a remarkable woman she had proven to be. And equally remarkable was the fact that he missed her so damn much, he could hardly wait to see her.

A few minutes later, Dale's private cell phone rang. He answered promptly, expecting his mother. "Hello?"

"I'm a journalist, Mr. Redington," came an unfamiliar voice." My name's Dan Casserly and I'm calling at the request of Sara Bowman."

"Is she all right?"

"She's fine — got a minute?"

Dale sat back in his chair. "Yes — all the time in the world for a friend of Sara's. What's up?"

Cas gave a modest summary of his background, explained that his fiancée, Hallie, was Sara's housemate, then quickly told Dale what little he knew about Jenna Snow's disappearance. He had many questions, but was willing to investigate and promised to keep everything confidential.

"But why would you work on a story you can't write about?" asked Dale.

"Because the woman I love asked me to call you. Because I enjoy solving mysteries. And because little babies need their mommies."

Dale burst into laughter. "Well, that's good enough for me. I'll tell you the whole story. Please keep track of your expenses so I can reimburse you. Got a pencil?"

"I'm at my computer, Mr. Redington."

"The name's Dale and here's what I know so far..."

— Chapter 33 —
The Next Day

"YOU MUST BE Mr. Redington," said a nurse Dale didn't recognize. "Sara's up in pediatrics. She wasn't sure when you'd be through with Dr. Cummings. I'll get her right away."

"Thank you." Dale took a chair opposite the main desk and glanced about. He hadn't paid much attention to the hospital's physical therapy center before, and was surprised to sense a fairly relaxed atmosphere.

One therapist passed by in mask and gloves, but most wore loose-fitting tops and pants and walked in and out the door without benefit of protective attire.

From where he sat, he could see into the main gym. The assembly of wheelchairs and walkers lined up by the entrance took him back to the time he and Daisy had been tourists at Lourdes.

The walls of the famous grotto had been packed with crutches, braces, splints and all sorts of devices owners had discarded as testament to their amazing "cures." Not a believer in miracles, Dale had wondered if they ever reclaimed them when the "cures" wore off.

"Sara's on her way, Mr. Redington. Would you come with me?"

He followed the woman down the hall to a treatment area similar to the one in the burn unit, only larger. On either side of the gleaming metal tub with its all-too-familiar chains, stretchers and pulleys, were three room-size booths. The attendant entered one and drew the curtain. "Sara thought you might want to wait here, where it's private. Would you like to lie down?"

"I'll sit, thanks. I'm fine."

A few moments later, the sound of heels clicking on the tile brought a tremor of pleasure. Incredible, he thought, how a few weeks of sightlessness had sharpened his sense of hearing. He'd know her footsteps anywhere.

"How's my best patient?" Sara pushed aside the curtain and breezed in, her eyes bright and welcoming. "I see Mitch has been working his magic. How do you like your new face mask?"

"I don't know," Dale said, rising. "I can't do much about what others see, but I can spare myself the shock."

"You haven't looked in a mirror? It's quite an improvement." She stood on tiptoe to examine his face, acutely aware that she was standing close to him, almost touching. For an instant, she found herself wishing he would wrap his arms about her — or at least, the arm not holding his cane.

A clear plastic shell covered his right cheek below the eye. "You're lucky," she said, backing away slightly. "These new face forms are a real improvement over the old ones."

"Is that where they get the name 'plastic' surgery?" he asked. Keep the conversation light, he told himself. Don't let her know how thrilled you are to see her. To his amazement and delight, he felt himself becoming aroused for the first time since the incident.

"I used to think the same thing," she smiled. "I was sure the name 'plastic surgery' came from the synthetics they use. But my brother Andrew taught me that it comes from *plastos*, a Greek word meaning to mold or shape."

"Didn't you say Andrew was a pediatrician?"

"Well, he would've been a plastic surgeon but Dad talked him out of it — convinced him he'd be crazy not to share his pediatric practice. So they work together now and Dad's thrilled — getting ready to retire in a few years."

Dale let her ramble on, as she continued to observe him and gently manipulate his arm. Her touch felt so good — so natural — so right. He wanted to let her know that she was exciting him with every movement. Professionally speaking, she'd be glad to learn that his sexual desire had returned. But he also knew that he looked horrible; she couldn't possibly be attracted to a man with half a face.

"I fired all my nurses yesterday," he said, unsure of her reaction.

"Good for you!" She chuckled. "You don't need nurses any more. As long as you have someone to cook your meals and drive you places, we can handle the rest right here. By the way, we had a staff meeting the other day and we all agreed your recovery's been amazing — almost miraculous. Now — suppose you sit down and let's slip off these elastic garments…"

— Chapter 34 —

AN HOUR OR SO LATER, Sara helped Dale into his tweed sport jacket. "You've been scrubbed, rubbed, oiled and exercised," she said, straightening his collar. "You should run smoothly for the next few days. When do you see Mitch again?"

"A week from today. My mouth goes under the knife. He's going to 'perfect my smile,' whatever that means."

"Just a tiny adjustment in the corner — right there. You hardly see it."

"Well, I'll be glad to have my lips functioning again.

He swears I'll be able to pucker, sneer and play the harmonica, even though I never could before. I may even be able to kiss again — assuming anyone would want to kiss a gink in a plastic mask and straitjacket."

"Quit fishing." She plucked a thread from his lapel. "You're a stunning looking man and you know it. A bit more repair work and you'll have all the ladies swooning again. Besides, your elastic garments bear no resemblance to a straitjacket."

"Tell that to my chest." His tone grew thoughtful. "When I first came home from the hospital, I swore I wouldn't have any more cosmetic surgery. But then I realized I was being selfish, sentencing the people I love, to look at this hacked-up puss for the rest of their lives. What's that old poem — 'My face I don't mind it because I'm behind it; it's the people out front that I jar'? So I decided to let Mitch finish his work."

"Dale," she said softly, "your face is looking good. Your features are in line. Nothing's distorted. You don't know how lucky you are. It's only those scars on your cheek that are going to be a challenge. And thank goodness you're being sensible."

"Thanks to you. You bolstered my confidence in Mitch — another reason I owe you."

"You don't owe me anything except to stay healthy. Mitch is an egomaniac, a sexual predator and a major ass-kisser, but he's the best there is when it comes to facial reconstruction. By the way, has he ever asked you for money?"

"Yes, he made a request." Dale rose and turned to

her. "He wants to build a new clinic."

"What did you tell him?"

"The same thing I tell everyone. Submit an application to the Foundation."

"You weren't upset?"

"Not at all. It's public knowledge that our family fund has a large grants budget every year. How would we know who needs help if no one asked?"

She stared a few seconds, then broke into a grin. "That's a relief. Mitch is a brilliant surgeon, but he's also a bit of a con artist."

"Then why would you want to work for him? He said you're going to be running his new clinic."

"He said what? That's totally false! The more I know about that man, the less I want anything to do with him!"

Sara was irate. Dale was such a dear, caring man. He badly needed someone to look after him and his airhead wife was never around. Maybe it was time he learned the truth about his beloved surgeon. "I wasn't going to say anything, but you should know this. I'm sure it was Mitch who gave you those extra drugs in the hospital."

Dale blinked in surprise. "Why on earth would he do that?"

"To keep you there longer, to keep you dependent on him so he could influence you and work on you for money. If I were you, I wouldn't give him a cent until we can check some things out. I'd warn your parents, too. The man can't be trusted."

Dale's eyes shone with gratitude. She was protective of him and didn't appreciate Mitch's lying to him. "In some ways I can take care of myself, Sara. In other ways, I need you — I need you very much."

His intensity communicated and she tried not to respond. Male patients often "transferred" to their physical therapists just as women often fell for their psychiatrists. She could almost recite the textbook: "Transference is the inappropriate transfer of feelings from the past... to a person or situation in the present."

And the counter-transference, she reminded herself, is equally inappropriate. Nevertheless, she reached up and touched the left side of Dale's face. "And I'm here for you, too, any time you need me."

PART 5

— Chapter 35 —

February, 2009

Daniel James Casserly, AKA Cas, breathed a long sigh, sipped his diet Pepsi and mopped his brow. He'd been working in Birdy's breakfast room since nine-thirty that morning and his stomach was growling.

Earlier, he'd made a stop next door. Fearful that the owner would start clearing out Shane's and Jenna's personal papers, Cas had accepted Birdy's offer to save and store them. At her request, he'd also helped her fold and transport the crib, as well as all of Vicky's possessions. No trace of a baby remained.

He had entered Jenna's house as if he owned it; nosy neighbors could be watching. Losing no time, he'd gathered up anything that might, even remotely, relate to Jenna's disappearance.

Now, despite feeling sure he was about to faint from hunger, he sat at Birdy's table, surrounded by mountains of files, clippings and documents.

Unlike his fiancée Hallie, he thought happily, Jenna was exceedingly verbose, at least on paper. She seemed to have an acute case of what Hallie called tossaphobia — fear of throwing anything away. Indeed, Jenna must have saved every note she'd written during her five years at the Golden Gate Star, and stored each in a folder, along with matching articles.

After going through the house, room by room, he'd learned that Jenna was also practical, frugal and surprisingly neat, considering the number of books, knick-knacks and pictures she'd accumulated.

Family photos covered half a wall in the bedroom. On the back of each, Jenna had written dates and the event, including her mother's and father's funerals. Childhood snapshots showed no siblings, only a timid young girl. Yet she seemed blissful in her wedding picture, short brown curls framing a round, youthful face, not pretty, but bright and lively. Freckles dotted the bridge of her nose and her mouth curled up shyly, framed in dimples. Her eyes gazed adoringly at her new husband.

Shane stood about a foot taller. Dark, shoulder-length hair, gray at the temples, made him look older and wiser. His nose pointed slightly downward, but he was smiling and clean-shaven. The overall effect was positive. In a masculine way, he was quite appealing.

A more recent photo showed Shane with fishing gear and his arm around a slightly shorter, bearded man, his brother Finnegan, identified by Jenna's caption on the back. The fraternal resemblance was unmistakable. Cas had slipped both pictures off the wall and into his briefcase.

In the small room Jenna used as an office, Cas had found bulging files of names, charity invitations, correspondence, PR contacts, story ideas, writers' bios and several copies of Shane's "Certificate of Death." The immediate cause, he noted, was "Cardiac Arrest," due to "Coronary Atherosclerosis."

Nowhere could he find Jenna's wallet, driver's license, credit cards, or any cash or jewelry. If someone *had* kidnapped her, and it was beginning to look that way, he had cleaned her out.

Shane's part of the house was limited to a single closet, a dresser and a desk piled with unopened mail. On top of the stack was a life insurance policy.

Without taking time to read anything, Cas had emptied the mail and the contents of the desk drawers into a plastic bag. Shane appeared to have little of value and he'd obviously taken his wallet with him on his fishing trip. If either Shane or Jenna had a computer, it wasn't there.

A last stop was their shared bathroom. Jenna's shelf in the medicine cabinet held aspirin, vitamins, birth control pills, eye drops, female hormones. The ledge above had shaving cream, aftershave lotion, Tylenol, ibuprofen and a near-empty bottle of yellow capsules. Since the container had no label, he'd stuffed it into the bag.

— Chapter 36 —

BACK AT BIRDY'S, Cas shut down his laptop, glanced at his watch and reluctantly declined Birdy's offer of an egg salad sandwich. Twenty minutes later, he was downtown, leaving his car in the Union Square Garage.

Walking swiftly, he made his way to the seventh floor of a nearby building, the newly remodeled offices of Citytalk. Published every other Monday, the magazine had started locally, but was recently bought by the Hellman Corporation, a national conglomerate.

Much to Cas's frustration, the recession had forced serious staff cuts at Citytalk, leaving only two people in management, three reporters, two people in production, one in distribution, four in advertising and sales and a young intern with an annoying crush on him.

"Executive editor" was his title, but Cas knew, as did everyone on the staff, that *he* ran the office. The publisher, when not out socializing and acting as figurehead for the magazine, spent much of his time flying back and forth from the capitol.

Grabbing a bag of stale peanuts and a Hershey bar from a drawer, Cas munched as he checked his emails, responded to the crucial ones, then picked up his iPhone.

Hallie answered immediately. "How'd it go?"

"That Jenna's a damn packrat," he said. "I haven't had time to look at Shane's papers yet. But if you've a few minutes to look over my notes on Jenna, I'll email them right away."

"I'll make time. Learn anything?"

"It looks as if foul play was involved. She's not the kind of woman who'd desert her baby. Thorough, detail-oriented, smart, she writes well, thinks clearly and cares about people and social issues. Many of her files deal with problems the Golden Gate Star would never take on. And no mention of her baby anywhere. Did Shane know she was pregnant?"

"No, according to Birdy, Shane died before she knew it herself. Then I think she took a leave right away. Maybe I should talk to Gretchen, the woman who replaced her at the Star."

"That would be wonderful. I spent way too long at Birdy's house. Nice lady and cute baby, but it means I'll be working till midnight."

"I won't wait up. Somebody loves you."

"Ditto," he grinned.

Hallie Marsh sat staring at her new Lucite-and-

107

chrome desk, a gift from her mother, a loving but domineering woman. In the mid-seventies, Hallie's late father had had the foresight to invest his wife's sizeable inheritance in French Impressionist paintings. The sale of a single Edouard Manet had allowed Edith Marsh to become a generous benefactor of the arts.

She doted on her only daughter, as well as her son, Robbie, who lived in Southern California. But she worried about Hallie, especially since Cas was Hallie's first romantic interest after her mastectomies. They had fallen in love before he knew about her surgery, and nothing had changed between them after he knew.

Edith Marsh's insistence that they wait two years to marry, was only postponing the inevitable.

Hallie smiled to herself as she ran her hand over the smooth acrylic surface. Lucite furniture was one of her weaknesses and she marveled at how well the desk fit in with her Charles Eames leather chairs.

Cas, a confirmed packrat, had once called her aversion to clutter "a real obsession." So what if it was? She loved the spacious all-white room with its lack of bookshelves, file cabinets, old newspapers, family pictures and the usual accoutrements of a bustling office. A single Dali watercolor adorned the wall behind a couch. Atop her desk sat a phone with an intercom, a computer, an external hard drive for backup, a printer and a few neat piles of paper.

The only decorative item was an acrylic frame that displayed a quote in calligraphy, a gift from Cas: "*Neatness is a virtue, but when carried to extremes, muddles the mind.*"

After spending half an hour studying Cas's notes,

she scribbled a list of questions, then remembered she'd offered to contact Jenna's replacement. The Golden Gate Star was not far from her office in the Financial District and the short walk, she decided, would give her time to think.

— Chapter 37 —

THE FASHION, PHILANTHROPY and society-oriented paper was headquartered in a sleek new downtown building, three stories up. The receptionist was excited to hear Hallie mention Jenna. "We really miss her, Ms. Marsh. I hope she's okay. I'll tell Gretchen you're here."

Moments later, a well-coiffed woman, designer-dressed, about 40, appeared and shook hands. "I'm Gretchen and I have five minutes," she said curtly.

Hallie smiled. "I'm not here on PR business. I'm trying to find Jenna Snow."

"Oh?" The woman's manner softened. "Then come into my office. I share it with the editor, but she's not here. Have a seat."

The crowded room hosted file cabinets and a large double desk. Framed covers of past issues filled the walls. A single window peered down on bustling Market Street.

Hallie perched on a chair; Gretchen sat facing her. "What's your connection with Jenna?"

"She and I have a mutual friend who's quite worried about her."

Gretchen looked puzzled. "It's a mystery. Everyone liked Jenna. She was a fine writer. She was at work, in fact,

109

when she got a call from Shane's brother, Finnegan Snow — can't forget that name! The brothers had gone salmon fishing in Kodiak — a small island in Alaska. Shane had apparently spent hours wrestling with a fish, then complained of chest pains. Finnegan took him on a helicopter to the nearest hospital — Anchorage, I think — and told Jenna it wasn't serious."

Hallie nodded her interest.

"But of course it was. Jenna came to the office the next day, distraught, as you can imagine. She told us Shane had had a massive heart attack that evening and died at the hospital within the hour. She said she couldn't afford to go to Alaska and fly the body home, so she asked Finnegan to have him cremated and bring back the ashes. They'd have a memorial service here."

"Did they?"

"I've no idea. Jenna stuck around a few hours to finish a story for the next issue. She was terribly upset. Our publisher told her to take two weeks off and tend to her affairs. Jenna seemed grateful, but for some reason, she deleted everything on her computer, as if she thought she might not come back. Yet she left all her books and files. The receptionist saw her leave the office about three, and that was the last we saw or heard from her."

"How strange!"

"We waited and waited, left phone messages, sent emails – no response. I was in sales at the time, but I have an editing background, so I filled in for her temporarily. After a few weeks, the publisher asked me to stay on as associate editor."

"Why didn't you send someone to her house?"

"We finally did, months later — me. No one answered her doorbell, so I rang the next door neighbor, Bertie-something. I told her we were going to report Jenna missing, but the neighbor said she was living with family in the east. That pissed me — we'd all been so worried. So I asked Bertie to come down to the office and pick up Jenna's things."

Several possibilities struck Hallie. "Did Jenna seem distressed over her husband's death?"

Gretchen paused. "She was upset, as I said, but she wasn't really grieving."

Funny, Hallie thought. Birdy had told Sara they had a good marriage. "Did you ever meet Shane?"

"He came into the office once — good-looking and quite charming. Seemed to be Mr. Nice Guy. Jenna told us he worked for an adoption lawyer, traveling all over the country trying to find pregnant women or new moms willing to give up their babies. He was away a lot, so Jenna would stay long hours working on stories."

"For other publications?"

"Mostly for the *East Bay Times*. They liked her articles." She paused a few seconds, then went on, "Ours is a lifestyle newspaper: charity events, beauty, fashion, décor, safe topics. We stay in our niche. Jenna was into social issues like human sex trafficking. She did a scary interview with a teenage girl who was kidnapped from her own driveway, drugged and forced into prostitution. Jenna published it under a nom de plume."

"What name did she use?"

"I don't remember. I'm sure it's in her papers, if the neighbor still has them. I also remember Jenna saying that after the story appeared, her editor got threatening phone calls. That's all I know. Now it's your turn."

"I'm afraid I don't know much — except that Jenna didn't go east to see her family. Birdy was mistaken. Unfortunately, she seems to have disappeared without a trace."

Gretchen frowned. "I'm so sorry! What can I do to help?"

"Nothing at the moment," said Hallie, rising. "But you've given me some ideas. Thanks so much for your time. I'll keep you posted."

— Chapter 38 —
A Month Later
March, 2009

A LARGE BROWN ENVELOPE from Eliva, the Cossa Clinic, finally appeared in Sara's mail box. An attached note apologized for the delay, explaining that the new brochures had been late arriving from the printer.

The twelve page folder was slick and colorful; at first glance, Eliva looked more like an upscale resort than a hospital. Watching the video, Sara saw the facility had impressive technology as well as luxurious grounds and décor.

Despite the frills, an interview in the brochure showed Dr. Cossa to be genuine and straightforward, and obviously proud of his clinic and its reputation. No prices were mentioned, so they had to be exorbitant.

The booklet offered practical facts and data, and

after a careful reading, Sara reassured herself that the director and his staff had impeccable credits. That, of course, could be checked with other physicians.

The clinic's approach, the brochure explained, was up-to-date, yet on the conservative side: "Employing the newest and best equipment in the world, we strive to maintain the highest standards of traditional surgery, combined with the latest discoveries in reconstructive techniques, scar removal, pain management and rehabilitation. Our goal is to renew the whole person as well as to heal the body."

Their twelve year record of successful cases was impressive, as were the before-and-after photos. Unlike Dale, most patients had come to the clinic badly disfigured. If Dale were to go there, he would have already undergone extensive corrective surgery. Only the deep scars remained.

The chances of him flying off to Wisconsin to be treated by a team of strange doctors, she realized, were zero to none. Still, it wouldn't hurt to send him the brochure, would it?

After making copies of the important pages, she packed the pamphlet in a plain envelope, stamped it, and before she could change her mind, walked to the corner and mailed it.

— Chapter 39 —

WHILE DALE recuperated at home, Sara Bowman was never far from his thoughts. What kept him from expressing them was the fact that he was still married, still needing therapy and still aware of his facial disfigurement. His amorous feelings were a fantasy to be enjoyed only by himself.

On the first Tuesday in March, Dale arrived at the hospital for his weekly appointment with Mitch, followed by his physical therapy session. Having survived successful mouth surgery, he seemed to be getting stronger and healthier with each visit.

Entering the physical therapy center, he saw Sara awaiting him at the nursing station.

"Great news," he said, approaching her excitedly. "Mitch just discharged me. No more skin grafts, no more surgery. I can't believe it!"

She stared at him in surprise. His face was truly remarkable; his eyes were wide and even, his smile warm and natural. Even his skin looked smooth and unblistered, except for four deep gashes on his right cheek. Mitch had done a remarkable job, but he couldn't possibly leave him unfinished. "I don't understand. What about — ?"

"The scars? Mitch says we should wait six months to a year and give them time to heal completely.

An alarm bell rang in Sara's head. "It's already been four months since your cheek surgery. And the scars have gone through all the usual color changes. The angry red has faded and they match your skin now, a good sign. Why doesn't he finish your face and be done with it?"

"I'm sure he has his reasons. I'll wear camouflage in public so little kids don't go screaming to their mothers." He pulled a large square dressing out of his pocket and held it up to his cheek. This will work, won't it?"

"No. It won't!" Her eyes flashed angrily. "Why should you go through that nonsense when he can fix those scars right away? I've seen him do it for other patients."

"Hey, look —" His face clouded with confusion. "If I'm not worried and Mitch isn't worried, why are you so upset?"

"Because I smell something unkosher. Is Mitch in his office?"

"He was when I left him a few minutes ago. But you can't —"

"Oh, yes I can. You're *my* patient, too, and I'd like to know what's going on. Start pressing down on that rubber ball, please. I'll be right back."

— Chapter 40 —

ANGER WAS WELLING UP in Sara as she took the stairs two at a time, promising herself not to let her feelings for Dale show. A physical therapist wasn't supposed to question the orders of a surgeon, especially the head of the department, but at the moment, she didn't care.

A knock on Mitch's door brought the emergence of a pretty young nurse, fumbling with her hair and looking flustered. Seeing Sara, she blushed brightly and hurried off.

"It's your body," Sara thought, not without compassion. Mitch had the ability to make every female think she was the most desirable being on earth.

"Am I disturbing you?" She peered into the office. His walls of framed certificates brought a silent chuckle. "Never be impressed by sheepskin," her father had told her. "Every time a doctor passes a urine test, someone hands him a diploma."

"You can disturb me any time." Oozing his usual charm, Mitch came around his desk. A surgical mask dangled from his neck, his starched blue scrub suit was clean and unwrinkled, and the scent of French cologne mingled with fumes of disinfectant. His eyes were caring and earnest as he took her hands. "Do you have any idea what you do to my respiratory rate? Why haven't I seen you lately? Have you been ignoring me?"

"We've both been busy," she said, pulling gently away. "May I sit down? I have a question — about Dale."

"Yes, yes, have a seat. You know, if you persist in running around this hospital looking so maddeningly adorable, I'm going to arrest right in front of you one of these days and you'll have to resuscitate me."

"I don't do mouth-to-mouth on doctors."

He grinned. "I love that sassy tongue of yours. Seriously, Sara, I've been meaning to tell you what a splendid job you've done with Dale. He's walking straight and tall, even starting to swing his arm a little. The family's very pleased with his progress and so am I."

"You're the one who's worked miracles. His facial recovery is amazing. It's the best reconstructive work I've ever seen."

"A compliment? From you? I shall treasure it until my deathbed. But I've the feeling you didn't come here to toss bouquets."

"No." She moved to the edge of her chair. "Dale told me you discharged him. I don't understand why you aren't removing his scars."

A flash of annoyance crossed the surgeon's features.

"I explained that very carefully. Resurfaced skin is at a high risk of becoming permanently discolored if we operate before it's completely healed. We're giving Mother Nature six to twelve months to work her miracles. If the blemishes hold their color till then, I'll fix them."

"But with all due respect, Mitch, those are deep, disfiguring scars. They appear to have healed as much as they're going to. And while he's waiting for this miracle, he's supposed to walk around with a big brown bandage on his face?"

"Are you questioning my judgment?"

Don't get hostile, she reminded herself. "Everyone knows you're a remarkable reconstructive surgeon, probably one of the best in the world. I just want a logical answer."

"And I gave you one, even though it's none of your bleeping business. Now — aren't you curious about our project?"

Not in the least, she wanted to say and he had no right telling people she would be involved. Working with him, if his new clinic ever materialized, was an idea she had toyed with briefly and discarded. His mammoth ego, his unbridled ambition, his insatiable libido — would only fill her life with problems. "Were you able to get funding?"

"I've applied and sent the papers. The Redington trustees meet and discuss applications all year long, but they don't make their final decisions till September. In the meantime, we'll just have to cross our fingers and pray."

September, she quickly calculated, was a little over six months away. "That wouldn't have anything to do with your decision to put off Dale's surgery, would it?"

"What are you talking about?"

She was tired of his chicanery. "Maybe — you're reluctant to release Dale. Maybe it was no accident that he got addicted to his medication and had to stay extra time in the hospital. And now you're making him wait for this surgery. As long as he needs that final operation, you've got him and his family dependent on you. And you're not about to give that up until you get what you want."

He glowered at her, his face contorted in anger. "How I treat my patients is none of your Goddamn business! If you value your job and your reputation, you'll shut your damn mouth and butt out of matters that don't concern you. Is that clear?"

Her brain seethed with comebacks. What about his reputation? Half the women in the hospital could charge him with sexual harassment. But she had nothing to gain by getting fired and Dale needed her to be there. For the moment, that was all she cared about. With pursed lips and a silent nod, she rose and walked out the door.

— Chapter 41 —

THE STEEL RAILING was so near and yet so far. Dale's right hand made a valiant effort, but he couldn't grasp it. He'd hoped to surprise Sara when she came back from seeing Mitch, but his fingers wiggled in vain, like fish trapped in a net. Fortunately, she had promised him the problem was temporary. With diligent work and exercise, he would someday be able to use his badly burned right hand to write, drive a car, play songs on the piano, and perhaps, even to caress a lady.

But someday was a long way off and the slow, painful recovery process called for more patience than he had — or would have had, without Sara. His mind sailed into a favorite fantasy: he was free again, a single man. His face and body were healed, and he and Sara were strolling in a country meadow. Her hair billowed in the breeze and she was laughing. They stopped to rest in the shade of a tree. He folded his jacket into a pillow, they lay down on the grass and before he knew it...

With effort, he switched off the scene he had no business imagining and attempted to rotate his elbow. Her voice rang through his brain like a recording: "Don't complain about what you can't do, be glad for all the things you can do."

Mindful of her encouragement, he tried again to curl his fingers around the bar. His lack of motor control was frustrating and made him want to grab his cane and leave. But he couldn't walk out on her, any more than he could deprive himself of her precious company. Bad enough that her superiors had dropped his sessions down to one hour instead of two. But she ignored them and still kept him the full two hours. He dreaded the day she would tell him he no longer needed her.

"You seem to be bending more easily." Sara walked over to the railing and flexed his arm. "Does this hurt?"

"Not when you do it," he smiled. "That was a quick visit. Did you see Mitch?"

"I saw him."

"And?"

"Frankly, I don't buy his explanation. Tell me if this hurts." She began to knead his fingers. "He expects you to live with those scars for the next six to twelve months and it's not right for you — either physically or emotionally. He should operate now and free you from him. But he wants to keep you dependent and — oops, sorry!"

His sudden intake of air made her lighten her touch. "Now raise your arm — easy. Try to make a fist. That's good. Dale, I'll be honest with you. I think you need a fresh pair of eyes. Perhaps you should get another surgical opinion. Would you consider it?"

"What about Mitch? Isn't he the best there is?"

"Technically, yes, but sometimes his ambition overrides his judgment. He doesn't have to know you're talking to someone else, and if he finds out, so what? You're free to get a second opinion. Let me do some research, first."

"Well — all right, Sara, I trust *your* judgment. But keep in mind that Mitch has been wonderful to me. I'd be very reluctant to leave him."

An hour or so later, Sara watched Dale unwrap the sterile dressing Mitch had given him, then helped him tape it to his cheek. What garbage, she thought, as she watched him walk off with that big, ugly bandage. Whatever Mitch was up to, he wasn't going to get away with it.

Home that evening, Sara lost no time calling her father and getting the names of two reconstructive surgeons he trusted. She phoned and spoke to both. Each gave positive reports of Eliva, as the Cossa Clinic was better known, and praised the physician who headed it. Antonio Cossa's reputation was legendary and those who could afford him were generally thrilled with the results.

Both surgeons agreed that a burn patient's scars needed time to heal, but that wearing a heavy face bandage for six months could pose emotional problems. Every case was different, they said, and the patient should take the advice of his doctor.

PART 6

— Chapter 42 —

March, 2009

SOFT CRIES from the crib awakened Birdy Silbert shortly after six the next morning. She rushed into the next room to find Vicky had kicked off her covers and seemed feverish. Cradling the baby, Birdy tried to soothe and quiet her, but Vicky pushed away her pacifier and cried even louder.

Concerned and frightened, Birdy remembered Dale had told her that if she ever had a problem, to call his physical therapist at St. Paul's Hospital. Fortunately, she'd scribbled the woman's name on a Post-It.

The hospital, however, was no help. "The physical therapy center is closed," said the weary switchboard operator, "Call back after eight." Birdy hung up, thought a few seconds, then dialed again and got a new operator. Pretending to be a relative, she explained that she needed to talk to Sara Bowman immediately about a family crisis. The operator noted her anxiety and promised to do her best.

Vicky was still sobbing ten minutes later when the phone rang. "Birdy, it's Sara. What's wrong?"

"I hate to bother you, but Vicky's got a fever and she won't stop crying. She needs to see a doctor, but if I take her to the hospital, I'm scared they'll ask questions and take her away from me."

"Calm down, Birdy. We won't let that happen. How old is she now?"

"Seven months and crawling on her tummy — getting into everything."

"How long will it take you to put her in a car seat and drive to St. Paul's?"

"Half an hour."

"Good. I'll meet you in the Emergency Room.

Don't talk to anyone or do anything till I get there."

Fortunately, the Emergency Room wasn't crowded at 6:45 a.m. and Sara was waiting. She helped Birdy sign in as Vicky's guardian and sped her through the red tape. A doctor came quickly, took about four minutes to discover that Vicky was teething, but otherwise, seemed in perfect health. He showed Birdy how to gently rub her gums, gave the baby a pain reliever, suggested rubber teething rings and acetaminophen and released them.

— Chapter 43 —

AT BIRDY'S near-insistence, Sara followed her home and went inside for a short visit. The "décor" was exactly as Dale had described it — kitschy and warm, overflowing with bric-a-brac, leafy plants and flea market furniture.

Happy to have her sore gums numbed by medication, Vicky nibbled on a pacifier as Birdy set her down in her crib.

"I thought maybe she was teething," Birdy ventured, "but I panicked when she wouldn't stop crying. Don't know what I would've done without you."

"You did the right thing." Sara tickled Vicky's tummy and got the hint of a smile. "What a beauty she is! Was her mother pretty?"

"Mmm — Jenna didn't care much about appearance. She lived in jeans and a T-shirt and almost never wore makeup. She was always worrying about some needy cause. Have you and Dale learned anything?"

"Not yet. As you know, I'm working full time and Dale's still healing from his last surgery, so my roommate and her fiancé offered to help us."

"Oh yes. That nice man Cas, who came to look at Jenna's papers." Birdy tucked the blankets around Vicky, now dozing contentedly. "Let's go in the kitchen. Have you had breakfast?"

"I have and I'm afraid I'm due at the hospital."

"Dale tells me he's doing well — thanks to you. He says he just needs one more operation. When will that be?"

"I'm not sure." A sudden thought flashed. "Birdy – just between us, I'm a bit concerned. Mitch, his doctor, wants him to wait six months before he operates on the scars and I don't think it's necessary. Dale needs to get on with his life, not wear a big bandage on his face for another half year. But he's reluctant to get a second opinion."

Birdy smiled. "Dale's very loyal."

"That's the problem." Sara checked her watch and spoke quickly. "He'll listen to you, Birdy. Next time you talk to him and he tells you he has to wait six months for the scar removal, would you kind of casually ask why he has to wait so long?"

"I certainly will! That would depress anybody and he's been through enough."

"Exactly! And let me know what he says." She searched her purse for a card, handed it to Birdy and gave her a hug. "Here's my phone number. You're as wonderful as Dale says you are."

— Chapter 44 —

LIFE HAD its moments, Dale Redington mused, grabbing a book and settling into his armchair for the evening. The second floor study was his favorite room in the house, perhaps because it was, uniquely, his room.

The walls were crowded with shelves of art books and first editions, the built-in cabinets housed his classical records and the Mason & Hamlin player piano he'd found at Bonhams & Butterfields' Auction Gallery was a favorite treasure. He liked plunking out the few songs he knew, but now that the electric mechanism worked, he could "play" it for hours, watching the ivories bob up and down by themselves, as if invisible fingers were hitting the keys.

Setting down his book, he reached on a table for the day's mail. A brown envelope with no return address caught his eye. Shaking out its contents, he found a colorful brochure with a Post-It on the cover. It read simply: "FYI - Sara."

Strange, he thought, scanning the pamphlet, that she would send him info about a fancy-looking burn center in Wisconsin. Surely she wasn't suggesting he fly some 2,000 miles for a second opinion — or was she?

Either way, it didn't matter. Perhaps Mitch had a few personality flaws, but he was a gifted and attentive surgeon. Sara's suggestion that he abandon the man who had spent so many hours painstakingly rebuilding his chest and face made no sense.

Daisy had left early that evening to attend a gallery

opening with friends, she'd told Dale, not bothering to name the friends — or the gallery. They were leading separate lives these days and for the moment, it didn't seem to matter.

She was out most of the time, and he'd reached the point where he no longer cared whom she was seeing.

Meanwhile, he had a plan. He was, as the Gershwin song goes, biding his time and living for Tuesdays, when he would see Sara at the hospital. His affection for her continued to intensify, and he longed for the day when he would be able to confess his feelings. That day, he prayed, would come soon — but he had to be patient.

Waiting, however, wasn't easy. He rarely stopped thinking about Sara during the day, and had to restrain himself from calling her at night.

He was, after all, a married man; telling his feelings would put a burden on her. Besides, he had no right to ask her to wait. The possibility that she would be scooped up by some handsome young intern was a risk he had to take.

"Damn!" he growled. His immediate problem was a torn fingernail. He rose, searched his desk for a nail file and not finding one, decided to check down the hall. Though he and Daisy generally stayed out of each other's rooms, the nail was distressing him and he was sure she had a manicure set.

Jars, bottles, tubes, brushes, makeup sponges and three mirrors with different magnifications covered the top of her dressing table. Rolling his eyes, he opened a drawer and found more cosmetics — spares, he guessed — then tried a second drawer. Soaps, creams, body lotions, but nothing for nails. The bottom drawer, to his surprise, was locked.

What could be inside, he wondered, trying to jiggle it open. Porn films? A secret recipe? A map to hidden treasure? It wouldn't be cash or jewelry. She kept those hidden in a wall safe.

His curiosity piqued, he glanced about the room and saw a large black leather bag – for daytime, he assumed, since she carried those small jeweled animals at night.

Rummaging through the purse, he pulled out a ring of keys. Ignoring the ones for the front and back doors, he tried all the others, but none fit the mysterious lock.

Undaunted, he put the keys back where he'd found them, and was about to close the purse when he felt a zippered pocket with something inside…another key!

Almost afraid of what he might find, he tried it in the lock. A turn, a click, the drawer opened! His immediate reaction was disappointment — nothing but a stack of papers. He chose the one on top, unfolded it and saw a familiar logo — Mitch's hospital stationery! Then, with an anxious heart, he began to read the handwritten scrawl.

— **Chapter 45** —

THE WORDS hit Dale like a bombshell. All the suspicions and anxieties he'd been denying for the past four months, all the hints he should have picked up, but told himself he was imagining — there they were — tangible, palpable, in black on white.

A deep sense of betrayal came over him. The object

of his despair wasn't only Daisy, whose flings and flirtations he'd known about, but now, he had to face the truth about his trusted friend. Where was the doctor's conscience? A man with Mitch's looks and magnetism could have almost any female he wanted, so why choose a married woman? Why choose his woman?

The first letter dated back to November, when he'd been lying sick and sightless in the hospital. Anger mingled with nausea as he read, *"My Darling Dearest Daisy, Last night was the most wonderful night of my life. Holding you in my arms, marveling at your beautiful firm breasts and flawless skin, caressing your soft, pink..."*

And on it went, in explicit detail. A quick run to the bathroom and Dale heaved into the commode. Twice. It helped. His temples throbbed, his heart pounded.

Experience had taught him there was a half-second interval when he could either give in to his rage and throw a tantrum, or talk himself back to sanity. He chose to try the latter. Anger without rage was manageable. Talking quietly to himself, he flushed the toilet, cleaned the bathroom and returned to the open drawer.

This time, he took a sheet from the bottom of the pile. Same logo, same scrawl, dated only two days prior: *"My Beloved Angel, I got your letter and of course I understand. I'm as anxious as you are that we be together forever, but we must be patient. Ellen is a good woman, even though she isn't good for me, and I don't want to hurt her or the children unnecessarily, just as I know you don't want to hurt Jimmy.*

We must wait till Dale is healed, then blame your

leaving on his burns and disfigurement, and how they changed his personality so he became bitter and abusive.

We must be practical so you don't walk away from your marriage with nothing. You deserve generous compensation for all the years of suffering..."

The letter ended, *"As I keep reminding you, it's imperative that no one find out about us. We must be even more discreet and meet every other week. Know that I love you with all my heart, my dearest, and we'll soon be together for the rest of our lives. As always, BTL. Mitch"*

All the letters ended with those initials. What the hell was BTL? "Drop dead, you lousy bastard!" Dale shouted, not caring who heard him. So much for control. He forced himself to sit down, take a series of deep breaths and count backwards from fifty. Then he checked his watch. It was still early. Daisy rarely came home before midnight.

It took the better part of an hour for Dale to copy each letter and return the pile to the drawer, leaving it, he hoped, exactly as he'd found it. Dropping the key in its zippered pocket, he replaced the purse on her dresser. Then, wondering if Mitch was hiding a similar pile of Daisy's letters somewhere, he walked briskly back to his study.

— **Chapter 46** —

A CUP OF TEA helped calm Dale's agitated stomach. His first impulse was to call Sara, but that could wait. For the moment, he had to go slowly, keep his cool and behave in public as if nothing had happened. But one matter could not wait. He reached for the phone.

"Dad, it's me."

"You sound out of breath. Are you all right?"

"I'm fine. Listen, our Foundation meeting tomorrow? I know one issue up for discussion is Mitch's application for funds for his clinic. I've learned that this would not be a good idea and I'm going to ask that we put his request on the back burner. I'm looking into another project that would be better use of our funds. Will you support me?"

A surprised silence. "Yes, of course. But what's he done?"

"Nothing to do with my surgery."

"Is it Daisy?"

The question startled Dale. "Ummm — actually, uh, yes. How did you — ?"

"Your mother and I aren't blind, son. Come in early tomorrow and we'll talk."

After thanking his father for understanding, and sending hugs to his mother, Dale tried to continue reading, but the urge to call Sara was too strong. He sighed with gratitude as she picked up the phone.

"Sorry to disturb you — it's Dale. I wanted to thank you for sending that brochure."

Her voice was soft and reassuring. "You never disturb me. In fact, I was just thinking about you. How're you doing?"

"Frustrated that it's Wednesday and I have to wait almost a week to see you."

A short pause. "Pretty soon, you may not see me at

all. Mitch says I get too attached to my patients, even though he's the one who ordered me to give you special attention. He told me Tuesday will be your last visit to the hospital. He wants to send his personal trainer to your house to continue your workouts."

How predictable, Dale thought. Mitch can't have Sara, so he's jealous of anyone else. Or maybe Daisy put him up to it. Sara would be mighty strong competition to have around.

"Are you too attached to your patient?" he asked.

"You know I'm very fond of you, Dale. But it has to end there. Circumstances —"

"Circumstances change." He caught himself. "What I mean is, I think you may be right about my needing a second opinion. Birdy suggested the same thing when I told her I had to wait six months. I'm considering that clinic — uh, in the brochure. What do you know about it?"

Hooray for Birdy, she thought. "The place sounds fabulous. I checked with several plastic surgeons and they all say Dr. Cossa works miracles with burn patients. But... you were so worried about hurting Mitch. What changed your mind?"

"I need to get away. I need time for myself. I think he'll understand."

"He'll probably blame me."

"Do you care?"

She laughed. "Not really. I have to change hospitals, anyway. He'll make my life miserable until I either sleep with him or agree to work in his new clinic. And both make me want to upchuck."

He wished she'd used a different word. "I've an idea," he said, as if it had just occurred to him. "How about if I hire you as my own private PT? Then you could quit your job and come to the clinic with me."

She laughed again. "Oh, Dale, I wish I could. But Daisy doesn't like me — and Mitch would have a heart attack. I guess the main thing is that it wouldn't be ethical. We're trained *not* to get emotionally involved with our patients. I could lose my license."

So she is emotionally involved. He grew bolder. "Would it be unethical if I asked you to have lunch with me?"

"Well, the asking isn't unethical, but the doing might be." Footsteps sounded in the background and her voice suddenly became impersonal. "Thanks for all the good news. Let me know how it works out."

Her discomfort communicated. "Sara, is someone there?"

"Yes, Hallie just came in. Sleep well and have a good night."

— Chapter 47 —

"WHO WAS THAT?" asked Hallie, setting her purse and briefcase on the kitchen counter. "As if I didn't know."

"Dale called me about a health matter."

"Yeah, sure. Get over him, dumb-bunny. Married men are the pits."

"I know. But if things were different..."

"They're not. And the blonde he married — Ditsy?"

"Close enough."

"Ms. Ditsy isn't about to let her rich hunk get away."

Sara pretended indifference. "What brings you to your second home tonight?"

Hallie perched on a stool. "Cas had to attend a dinner. By the way, I stopped by Birdy's house after work. Nice woman. I went through some of Jenna's papers. Those free lance articles she wrote for the East Bay Times, wow — she had guts!"

"Scary?"

"Yes. One story said that the Bay Area's become a hotbed of human sex trafficking. Young women and children are being kidnapped and sold into slavery right here, under our noses. Terrifying stuff! Jenna was thirty-eight, too old for the sex trade. But not too old to do an exposé."

"That *is* scary."

"What if some of those horrible people read her story and decided to shut her up? She was also looking into illegal adoptions and baby brokers — creeps who buy and sell black market babies. Gretchen, the woman who replaced her at the newspaper, said that Jenna's husband, Shane, had a job finding unwanted babies for adoption. I wonder if he was part of that underground. I'd like to talk to his boss, a lawyer named Cyril J. Greenfield."

For a few seconds, Sara seemed lost in thought. Then she spoke. "What if Jenna was so secretive about her pregnancy because she thought the bad guys might try to steal her baby?"

"My thoughts exactly. It's all starting to tie together

— the kidnapped girl, the copious notes on baby brokers. Gretchen said that after Jenna's story on sex trafficking ran, the publisher at the East Bay Times got threatening letters."

Hallie hopped off the stool and grabbed her briefcase. "Stay tuned — more to come. Sorry to talk and run, but I need some clothes, then back to my love nest."

"Ok. But don't forget what your mother told you. No sex till you get married."

"At least my guy isn't already married."

"Touché." Sara laughed and blew a kiss.

— Chapter 48 —

"FORGIVE THE CLICHÉ," said Cas, hugging Hallie as he entered his apartment later that night, "but it is a damn small world!"

"Bet you ran into an old girlfriend. Which one of the thousands?"

"Ah yes, all those years of meaningless encounters… I was just looking for you, my sweet. And no, this *was* an attractive young woman, but we've never met before. Her name is Isabelle Lee. She works as an English second language tutor to Chinese students. She also makes beaded purses — I almost bought one."

"Are you trying to tell me something?"

"Absolutely. She sat across from me at dinner. I admired her bag and she gave me her card in case I wanted to order one for my wife. I teasingly asked what she was going to do with all the money she made. She said she was saving to buy a crib set for her baby, due shortly. Then she would buy a gift for a man who'd risked his life for her."

Hallie sighed. "Bottom line?"

"Patience, my love, is a virtue. And one you charmingly lack. Do we have to stand here in the hallway?"

Taking his hand, she led him to a couch in the next room, sat down beside him and placed his arm around her. "Okay. Now talk."

He laughed and squeezed her closer. "I sensed a story, so I got her to tell me…about the stranger who was driving by and saw her house on fire. She came dashing out and begged him to save her grandfather. The Good Samaritan ran inside, rescued the old man, but couldn't save him and got badly burned. Sound familiar?"

Hallie drew back to stare. "Dale Redington?"

"None other! So I told this pleasant young lady that I'd had the pleasure of speaking with Mr. R. on the phone and planned to do so soon again. She asked me to find out if there was something she could get him — anything in the world she could do to show her gratitude. I said I'd think about it."

"While you're thinking, can we go to bed? It's been a long day and I'm too tired to tell you about it."

"Okay. Will you marry me?"

"That makes two hundred and forty-seven times you've asked."

"I know, but I like to hear the answer."

She giggled. "Let's go to bed and then I'll decide."

— Chapter 49 —

DISAPPOINTED THAT SARA couldn't accompany him to the Clinic, Dale lay back on his pillow and faced the fact that his fantasy had been just that — a fantasy. A married man did not go off for two weeks, or however long it would take to get rid of his scars, with a gorgeous unmarried woman, PT or not. But he had a plan.

First thing in the morning, he would ask his primary care Doc, Hadley Harris, to find out about the clinic. If the reports were positive, he'd phone and see when they could take him. The sooner he went, the sooner he could get his surgery and come back to Sara. And the sooner he could start to get out of his marriage, which he should have done years ago.

Jimmy, of course, was a problem. The boy was aware of his mother's failings, often made excuses for her and always stuck up for her. Walter Redington had hoped Dale could keep the marriage together till Jimmy went off to college, but Dale wasn't willing to wait.

He reasoned that Jimmy would be crushed no matter when his parents split, but he reassured himself that his son was highly sensitive and must have known that his Mom and Dad were not happy with each other.

Telling Mitch and Daisy about the Cossa Clinic, however, was his immediate concern — along with trying to act as if he didn't know what was going on with them. If he could pull that off, he'd deserve an Oscar.

The report from Dr. Hadley Harris came late the

next afternoon. Wisconsin seemed a long way to go, he thought, when Dale only needed one more operation. But yes, the clinic's reputation was tops and Dr. Cossa was something of a deity in the world of plastic and reconstructive surgery. To Dale's relief, Dr. Harris had a full waiting room and no time to ask questions.

Hearing the positive report, Dale immediately called Wisconsin. Speaking to Eliva's "concierge," he learned that he would first have to send all his medical records, plus two doctors' recommendations, be considered by Eliva's medical board, then their advisory board, then possibly, they might be able to take him in a few months.

His next call was to Mitch. "How's my favorite patient?" answered the cheery voice.

"Feeling good, thanks to you," Dale replied nervously. "I know your busy schedule so I'll get right to the point. The phone isn't the best way to tell you this, but I need to get away for awhile. I've heard about a clinic in Wisconsin with a funny name…"

"Eliva? The Cossa Clinic?"

"You know it?"

"Everyone knows Eliva. I plan to model *my* new clinic after it. Dr. Cossa is world famous…" His voice dropped. "But why do you need another surgeon, Dale? Have I been neglecting you?"

"No, not at all. I just have some personal problems to work out, away from the pressures at home. I haven't told Daisy yet — I'm hoping she'll come with me."

"Oh, well, that would be fine. You know, it's not a bad idea. With your brilliant brain, you could observe what they offer and come back with all sorts of ideas for me — if you could jot down a few notes on what they do right, what they do wrong, that could be of immense help to me. When do you plan on going?"

"I don't know yet. Wanted to get your input."

"I approve. It's a wonderful idea for you to get away for a while and recuperate in a caring atmosphere. When you come home, we can talk about doing your last surgery."

Dale felt a surge of relief. "In that case, would you mind sending them my medical records and a letter of recommendation? Do you need an address?"

"No. Wish I could go with you, but they wouldn't be thrilled to have a competitor hanging around. I'll have my nurse send off your records and we'll talk before you go. Be sure to take a camera. That's exciting news."

"Thanks, Mitch. Appreciate your help." Dale had to bite his tongue to keep from saying words he'd regret. Amazing that the doctor considered himself "a competitor." In his mind, the Redington Foundation's funding of his clinic was a *fait accompli.*

Sorry, Dr. Mitchell Cummings, Dale said to himself. Next time keep your friggin' pants zipped.

— **Chapter 50** —

HER ARMS LOADED with packages, Daisy Redington came home from a shopping spree to find her husband reading in the living room. He quickly closed his book and asked her to join him.

"Can't now, sweetie," she called, blowing him a kiss.

"Have to change my clothes — going to a movie with the girls."

"I only need five minutes, Daisy. Please?"

"Well, okay, five minutes." Setting her shopping bags on the stair landing, she approached him with a look of concern. "Are you feeling all right?"

"Fine. Did you pick up some nice bargains?"

"They weren't exactly bargains," she said, laughing. "But yes, they're nice. I found a blouse for my blue —"

"I don't care about that. I want to tell you about this burn clinic I'm thinking of visiting. It's supposed to be beautiful, like a very exclusive spa. It has all the newest technology and the latest of everything, including the world's best surgeons and burn specialists."

"Oh?" Instantly alert, she asked, "What's wrong with Mitch?"

"Nothing. In fact, I just talked to him and he agrees it would do me good to get away and get some new approaches to rest and rehab. I'd like you to come with me." He offered her the brochure. "Check it out."

She dropped to the couch beside him and glanced at the booklet, leafing through the pages. "It does look inviting," she said. "But why Wisconsin? We have lots of good spas in California."

"Nothing that compares to this. I think you'd enjoy it. You could get facials and massages…"

"When were you thinking of going?"

"As soon as they can take me — maybe next week, maybe three months — I don't know."

She handed back the leaflet. "If your heart is set on

going, Dale, then by all means, go. The committee asked me to chair the Holiday Gala again this year, so I'm afraid I couldn't go with you, much as I'd love to."

"Couldn't someone take your place?" For a short second, he almost hoped his marriage might be saved.

"No, there are too many details only I know about. You're better off going by yourself — I'd only be a burden and you'd worry about my being bored."

She was right. How could he possibly be so stupid as to think she really wanted to be with him. "Is that final — or open to discussion?"

"What's gotten into you?" she asked, stroking his cheek. "You're acting strange. Are you sure you feel okay?"

"Yes — thanks." He recovered quickly. His anger mustn't show. "I guess — this whole business has worn me down. I'm tired of pills, tired of not being able to drive or work, tired of the hospital and tired of looking at these damn walls."

"I understand. And Mitch thinks it's a good idea to go to this place in — Wisconsin?"

"Yes."

"Then you should go. How long will you stay?"

"I don't know that, either."

"Let's talk tomorrow." She glanced at her wrist and kissed his forehead. "I've got to change now. Michiyo made you something special for dinner."

And she was off.

Dale heaved a loud sigh. Both his wife and her lover seemed delighted to shoo him out of town. The situation was ludicrous, in a way, and playing games with people was not a practice he enjoyed. But his father had insisted he talk to the family lawyer before he let on to Daisy and Mitch that their "secret" was anything but.

And so, reluctantly, he went to see the attorney and they spoke of divorce. The fact that Mitch — in his own handwriting — was urging Daisy to get "generous compensation for all the years of suffering," as well as the accusation that Dale had become "bitter and abusive," was enough to fire up the lawyer's enthusiasm.

He would start with the paper work and file documents when Dale returned from Wisconsin. In the meantime, he warned Dale to confide in no one.

Two weeks passed before Dale learned that he would be most cordially welcomed at Eliva a month or so later, on the first of May.

PART 7

— Chapter 51 —

Late April, 2009

THE EVENING before Dale left for Wisconsin, he phoned Birdy Silbert to tell her where he'd be, then called Sara to say good-bye and asked her to keep him informed on the Jenna case. His parting words were, "Remember — I care about you." She had simply replied, "Me, too."

Not having seen her housemate lately, Sara phoned Hallie to convey Dale's message. The request inspired Hallie to take a break from her public relations business and devote the next day to her neglected project. After spending the morning poring over Jenna's files, notes and assorted papers, she learned several intriguing facts.

One was that Shane's employer, Cyril J. Greenfield, had a website. Among a long list of family services that included divorce, prenuptial agreements and estate planning, she noted, "Adoption." The explanatory passage read:

"Our firm specializes in finding good homes for healthy newborns. And while provocative pictures of needy infants in foreign countries are appealing, we have found that domestic adoption is far easier, faster, less complicated and more affordable. We are proud to have facilitated the private adoption of more than 300 American newborns.

"Our firm of nine legal experts spends a quarter of a million dollars annually to find birthmothers. Thus, we are able to provide legal adoption services all over the United States. We especially pride ourselves on our sensitivity and our respect for the privacy of all parties involved."

Copies of the Snows' joint tax returns showed that their annual income was small, and that Shane had been working for the lawyer when he died. His one — and perhaps only — function seemed to be to find unwed pregnant teenagers, rape victims, or any new mothers willing to part with their babies. Apparently, Jenna was checking the legality of all this when she disappeared.

A file also turned up Jenna's interview with the 15-year-old girl who was kidnapped from her driveway, drugged and sold into prostitution. The horrifying article, credited to "Marilee Kosovsky," indicated that Jenna was scared to use her own name. The story had run in the East Bay Times, and reported that two suspects were in custody.

Worse, yet, the two kidnappers were found guilty of the charges, but only got twelve years and could be out sooner on parole.

A follow-up by "Marilee Kosovsky" told how FBI agents had spotted the victim on a Craigslist ad, selling sex. Another website was offering girls as young as eleven to the highest bidder. Jenna's research showed that sex trafficking was far more lucrative than drugs.

Cyril J. Greenfield's name had come up in Jenna's notes on another subject — adoption, and the buying and selling of babies. She was frustrated that her husband, Shane, was evasive about his work and unwilling to discuss any aspect of it. Perhaps he had good reason. "Marilee Kosovsky" was getting ready to submit her next exposé — a serious assault on the burgeoning baby industry.

— Chapter 52 —

AFTER LONG PONDERING, Hallie still could not come up with a plausible reason to call Cyril J. Greenfield. Could she use a pseudonym? No, she told herself. This would be one shrewd attorney, who would probably check up on every word she told him.

After discarding a series of possible scenarios, she decided the best way to get to him would be to offer him something he wanted — and what he most wanted, it seemed, was babies.

She quickly vetoed the idea of pretending to be pregnant, then got distracted by an unhappy client — a restaurateur who wanted to cancel his PR contract. The recession was killing his business, he said. Hallie sympathized; hers was hurting, too. She would return his check.

A call from Cas came next. "I just phoned Dale," he growled. "The butler or whatever-he-is said, 'Mr. Redington's out of town and I don't know when he'll be back.' What-the-hell's going on?"

"Calm down, honey. Sara told me he was going to a burn clinic in Wisconsin to get a second opinion on his next surgery — and possibly to get away from his wife."

"Damn! How does he expect us to find Jenna when he's not around to help?"

"He hopes to be back in a few weeks. Sara said he sounded nervous about going, but asked her to explain the situation to you and me."

"Explain."

"She thinks he's having problems with Ditsy."

"Daisy," Cas corrected and paused to catch his breath. "Damn again! I had an idea I wanted to run by him."

"What idea?"

A phone jangled in the background. "Oops! Gotta go. More tonight."

— Chapter 53 —
That Evening, 2009

HALLIE STARED UP at the sign she'd hung over Cas's stove: *"Real Women Don't Cook"*

"Amen!" she mumbled, then proceeded to stir the instant turkey gravy she was about to pour over the instant mashed potatoes. She'd already nuked the frozen string beans and sliced the Trader Joe's smoked turkey breast. "Who says I can't cook?" she asked aloud.

Sounds at the door made her smile and quickly hang her plastic apron on a hook by the broom. "Is that you, Henry?" she called out.

"No, it's Harry," Cas called back. "Has your boy-friend left?"

"Sure. But you'll do." She greeted Cas with a kiss on the lips. "You're cute, you know?"

"All the girls tell me that." He grinned and un-loaded his briefcase. "Smells good. Had to skip lunch today. What's for dinner?"

"Shall we pretend we're married and gobble down the food in ten seconds while reading the newspaper? Or can we pretend to be civilized and take fifteen minutes for a quiet glass of chardonnay in the living room?"

"The former," he said, heading for the kitchen. "I'm starved."

Dinner was almost over when Cas set down his fork and turned to Hallie. "Want to hear the idea I mentioned on the phone?"

She nodded.

"It's simple. Suppose I put a notice and a picture in Citytalk offering a reward for information leading to the whereabouts of Jenna Snow. I bet Dale would put up five grand. We'd be swamped with clues!"

Hallie shrugged. "A while back, Dale offered to do that. I told Sara to tell him not to. It would alert the bad guys, or whoever hurt or kidnapped Jenna, that we're looking for them. It could defeat our purpose."

"You still feel that way?"

"Kind of. Advertising should be a last resort. What I really need is a reason to call on Mr. Greenfield, the lawyer. Shane worked for the guy, trying to find babies wherever he could. He had to know what Shane was up to."

Cas brightened. "I could get you pregnant."

"Next thought?"

"Isabelle Lee. Remember the lovely Chinese girl who wants to do something for Dale? She's already pregnant. She could go with you."

"What good would that do?" Hallie paused a few seconds. "Wait — what if she said — well, we wouldn't lie — but she could say she's having a baby and wanted to ask some questions. Is she married?"

"Let's hope so. How would that help us find Jenna?"

"It won't, but it might be a good place to start. Jenna suspected Shane's work was not kosher, and she was determined to find out whatever she could. She was deep into researching baby brokers — unscrupulous doctors, lawyers, unlicensed 'facilitators' such as midwives, bankers, even clergy. These brokers often procured infants from needy families and third world countries. Isabelle might be just what I need to get in the lawyer's door. Could you set up a lunch for three? Say I want to see her purses."

"Hal — I know I suggested Isabelle, but you're getting into dangerous territory. I don't like it."

"All we need to do is to see this lawyer and find out what he pays for babies, where he gets them and so on. We'd have no reason to see him unless we wanted adoption information. We'll imply, but we won't lie."

"I don't like it a bit."

"Set up a date, please? Pretty please? Sara's birthday's coming up and she desperately needs a new purse."

PART 8

— Chapter 53 —

May, 2009

THE CLEAR WISCONSIN sky was just beginning to darken.

"Awesome" was Dale's reaction to his first view of Eliva, a mini-city of marble-and-glass lit up on the banks of an emerald-blue lake.

Across the water, impressive mansions peeked out from behind towering trees and lush vegetation. Yachts of all sizes and styles, moored to private docks, swayed in the breeze. A few water skiers enjoyed a twilight run.

The uniformed driver who'd met Dale at the Appleton airport was happy to answer questions. Yes, the food at Eliva was excellent, the staff friendly and professional, the weather warm and mild, although, "We had 90 inches of snow last winter."

And yes, some of the guests *were* snooty, he admitted, but anyone who could afford to go there could afford to be snooty. "I didn't mean you, sir," he'd hastily added. "I'm sure you'll enjoy your stay. Everyone does."

"I'm sure I will — but getting here's rather a pain." Dale tried not to sound too cross. "An hour delay in the San Francisco airport, a three-hour flight to Chicago, then sitting around that airport for hours, and finally a forty-minute flight to Appleton. And we've been driving for over an hour now..."

"Yessir! You must be very tired. But please, don't miss the view. If you read the brochure, you know about our famous landscaping and architecture. We've won at least a dozen prizes. This is all Eliva property, except for Lake Minekka. Those are our cranes feeding in the field. And that's an eagle flying by — you don't see many of those in California."

151

"No, not many." Dale sighed and shifted his weight in the back seat, where the driver had insisted he sit. His right arm ached and his cheek itched under the heavy dressing. "What are those trees?"

"Pines, oaks. We used to have poison oak but it's gone. You can pick wild blackberries, raspberries. And your guide will give you a spray to scare off the mosquitoes. That's our national bird."

Dale laughed politely. "Tell me about Eliva. What's the origin of the name?"

"Yessir! It's a legendary city where people came from all over Europe to be healed — like Lourdes. The myth originated around 1150, when fires ravaged a city in Spain and there was an epidemic of third degree burns. It's also the name of a tropical town in Africa, but that's a coincidence. What we like is that Eliva is an anagram of 'alive.' "

Talk ended quickly as the driver passed a "Private Property; Authorized Vehicles Only" sign and turned into a roadway dwarfed by giant palms on both sides. Flowery branches wound around the tree trunks.

As the limo pulled up to the first building, two men in green suits and ties appeared in the entrance. They greeted Dale by name, helped him out of the car and offered a wheelchair.

"Thanks, I can still walk," he said, smiling.

"Just a courtesy, Mr. Redington. You seem in excellent health and you'll only get better."

"I'm counting on it."

The spacious white marble lobby housed a ten-foot long tank of tropical fish. Under a soaring ceiling, a large screen showed photos of blissful patients reclining on the grounds and enjoying its facilities. A portrait of a young Dr. Cossa stood out against slate gray walls.

Behind the Welcome Desk, where Dale signed in and showed his credit card, a round mohair couch and ikat-covered chairs formed a sitting area. Soft classical music warmed the air.

The scene was exactly what Dale had feared and worse — overdone, luxurious, built to impress, everyone gushing and solicitous.

He would last as long as he could.

— Chapter 55 —

"Mr. Redington," cooed a female voice. "Welcome to life-restoring Eliva. I'm Athena and I'll be your spiritual and physical guide. Would you like to familiarize yourself with Eliva before we go to the penthouse?"

He turned to face a strikingly beautiful brunette. A generous cleavage and abundant curves had been squeezed into a tight green dress. "Thanks, but I just need a bed. I'm pooped."

"Fatigue is the first step in the renewing process. Your bags are en route to your new home."

"Bag — singular," he corrected. "Hope we're not expected to dress for dinner."

"We have no dress code, Mr. Redington. You're free to dress as you please — and to do almost anything you please, as long as it's healthful, legal and thoughtful to others. We pride ourselves on our personal attention to each and every guest. We're here to please you, to pamper you, to revitalize your zest for living as we watch you heal. Major burns stress major organs, that's why we encourage a holistic approach that unites mind, body, spirit and environment. We believe your visit to Eliva will be an inspiring experience that will help you celebrate the miracle of life… forever."

She paused for emphasis, then turned to lead the way, leaving him a vision of a wind-up key in her back. How many times had she said that speech? And how many gullible guests had swallowed it? Her "personal attention" made him feel like a slab of meat on an assembly line. What was he doing in this phony atmosphere? Why had he come so far from home?

He quickly reminded himself. He'd had to get away from Daisy and Mitch, or surely, he'd have confronted them. He still needed medical care, still wore a bulky bandage over his cheek, but he no longer trusted Mitch. One careless move in surgery and Daisy would have been a very rich widow. He'd taken the precaution of changing his will before leaving.

Sara, too, seemed to have lost whatever respect she had for Mitch. Furious that he was spreading lies about her, she'd gone online, found the world's best burn center and encouraged Dale to seek it out. His first reaction had been to stay loyal to Mitch, but when faced with lies and betrayal, the picture had changed.

And how desperately Dale had wanted to take Sara with him. But not a good idea, she'd explained and her reasons made sense. How wise she was!

He wondered — had she sensed he was planning a divorce? Did she know how deeply he felt about her? Did she know about Daisy and Mitch? No question she knew. The whole hospital probably knew. He missed her already.

"And here we are," announced the talking robot, who hadn't stopped for breath all the way up in the elevator. "You'll rejoice in Shangri-La, Mr. Redington. It's our most exquisite suite."

"Call me Dale."

"Congratulations!" She clapped her hands so vigorously, he thought her breasts would pop out. "You've already tuned in to the warm family spirit of Eliva."

Custom-designed from the ceiling on down, gleaming and immaculate, "Shangri-La" was indeed stunning. A black granite bar faced sleek black leather chairs and a matching sofa. A small Steinway upright filled a corner of the sitting room. Atop it sat an ikebana floral sculpture. Nearby, French doors opened onto a private patio overlooking the lake.

"Welcome to your new abode, Dale. May I assist you to unpack?"

"No, thanks. If you don't mind, I'd like to be alone."

"I understand. Solitude frees the soul. Have a peaceful rest. If you need anything at all, touch the *petite boite* by your bed and someone will come to you instantly, twenty-four seven."

"*Petite boite*," he repeated. "Thanks."

Somewhat dazed and totally exhausted, he watched

her disappear down the hallway, closed the door and headed for the nearest bed.

— Chapter 56 —

THE STAY STARTED out slowly for Dale. Dr. Cossa had been in surgery for two days, but was able to examine him on day three. The famous doctor was unlike Mitch in every way. Short of stature as well as charm, he looked to be in his mid-sixties, with very little hair and a disdain for small talk. Bright eyes hid behind thick glasses, as he examined Dale's scars with frowning intensity.

Then, after checking Dale's medical history, he turned off the overhead spot and helped his patient sit up.

"Will I live, Doctor?"

"That is not the question. The question is — what are your expectations?"

"I'd like to get rid of these scars, if possible."

"It is definitely possible. Dr. Cummings did excellent work on you. Why did you leave him?"

"Personal reasons."

"Good. Nothing to do with his work. We'll talk more about what I can and cannot do for you after my staff gives you a pre-op schedule. Check at the desk."

And Dr. Cossa was gone.

Dale found the surgeon's paucity of words a welcome contrast to Athena's gibberish and was anxious to start whatever preparations he needed. The nurse begged him to be patient and scheduled him for a complete physical, including a stress test, and before-and-after-surgery visits with the nutritionist, psychiatrist, pharmacist, and physical therapist.

For the next ten days, he would be awakened for an early morning hike, fed a healthful fat-free, sugar-free breakfast, then offered a choice of some thirty different spa treatments. The list included: The Stone Age Bath (hot rocks applied to his naked body), the Golden Renewal (a 24-karat gold dust scrub to "stimulate cell regeneration"), a Terfezia (white truffle) Exfoliation Dip, a Cristal Champagne Soak in a copper tub, a Petrossian Caviar Coronation (to "relax the hair follicles"), and a Bladder Wrack Seaweed Wrap, whatever that was.

Along with those overpriced and highly creative offerings, there were mango-kiwi facials to shrink his scars, bee venom organic hair treatments, a "miracle foaming bubble skin repair" and even "a youth-restoring semen rub." (His own semen would be mixed with medicinal herbs and sponged over his body.)

Since Eliva's guests were supposedly free to do as they pleased, Dale enjoyed the fresh air walk before breakfast, but had no interest in getting crowned by caviar or wrapped in some creature's bladder. Aside from conventional burn medications and ointments, the only treatments he wanted were the doctor-ordered antibiotic facials and a plain old-fashioned Swedish massage or two, if available.

Athena tried everything short of helping him procure his semen, to convince him to "embark on a magical journey of exaltation and discovery," but he wasn't buying.

— Chapter 57 —

A TOUR OF THE GROUNDS was first on Athena's schedule. She showed Dale through the recently-built hospital, emphasizing its fully-equipped operating room with state-of-the-art life support, monitoring equipment and "spiritual ambiance."

She let him peek into the 15-bed intensive care unit with its independent ventilating system to avoid "earthly contamination." Nearby, he recognized the ultrasonic hydrotherapy equipment used for bathing wounds, as well as the hyperbaric oxygen chamber, said to reduce infection. He had experienced both.

On to the rehab section of the campus, where they visited the healing units, the art, music and play theater, the beauty and barber shop and the gym and physical therapy center. Just beyond were a swimming pool with "eco-friendly" cabanas, a Pilates fitness studio, tennis courts, golf course and Zen Sanctuary Garden.

Having seen (and heard about) it all, Dale planned his daily routine.

Charmed by the tea house in the Zen Garden, he'd begun to go there every morning after his hike and breakfast. Once he'd convinced Hubballi, the pleasant Indian caretaker, that he wanted to be left alone, he would sit on a bench by the lily pond, sip cinnamon tea and read till lunchtime.

Hubballi had insisted on giving him a copy of Alan Watts' classic *The Way of Zen*, written in the mid-50's. Dale recognized the lines of an old Zen poem, with its seemingly illogical reverses of common sense:

"The perfect Way (Tao) is without difficulty,
Save that it avoids picking and choosing.
Only when you stop liking and disliking,
Will all be clearly understood..."

The challenge to revisit the Buddhist philosophy he'd embraced in college, plus the pervasive quiet and beauty of the garden were all the emotional "renewing" Dale needed.

Afternoons, however, took him back to reality. The hours were filled with physical therapy treatments, exercises, one-on-one appointments with the dietician, the psychiatrist, the respiratory care practitioner, the Monday-to-Friday support groups.

At first he'd felt he had no need for the meetings, but after a few sessions, when he saw what horrors some of the other burn victims had experienced, he began to realize his good fortune at having survived almost intact.

One patient, a bilingual Frenchman in his thirties, had jumped from the roof of a flaming apartment building and suffered burns over ninety percent of his body surface, along with a fractured leg and crushed ankle. Hopital Foch in Paris had supplied oxygen, administered analgesics and IV fluids and placed him on mechanical ventilation. No one expected him to live, but after a ten-month treatment and recovery period, he surprised his wife and even his doctors, by surviving. At Eliva, along with the burn therapy, he was learning to walk again.

Energized by the young man's curious mind and will to live, Dale dropped the usual caution barriers and opened himself to a warm relationship. They shared long conversations on Zen Buddhism and almost every other subject, agreed, disagreed, challenged, teased, laughed and confided in each other as men rarely have the time or inclination to do.

Then, every evening after dinner, Dale would call Sara, who would catch him up on the day's happenings. He learned that Mitch was still planning on getting a grant from the Redington Foundation, and that Sara had passed his office one afternoon, heard loud arguing, and recognized Daisy's voice.

"Do you think something's going on there?" he'd asked innocently.

Sara had said, "What do you think?"

And he'd replied, "I really don't care anymore."

His answer allowed him to respect his lawyer's warning about keeping silent, yet still be honest with Sara. What was left unsaid…was understood.

PART 9

— Chapter 58 —

April, 2009

Isabelle Lee was the first to arrive at Mandalay, a popular Burmese restaurant on California Street. She was seated at the table when her hosts appeared, greeted Cas warmly and shook hands with Hallie.

"You didn't tell me how pretty she was," teased Hallie, noting their guest's long black hair and delicate Asian features. "But Cas did rave about your purse."

"I'm so glad!" Her face lit up. "I brought a few to show you."

"Let's order first," said Cas, beckoning a waiter. "I'm starved."

"He's always starved." Hallie turned to Isabelle. "Are you on a special diet?"

"Yes, I eat everything in sight." All three laughed.

"Good, then we'll let Mr. Casserly order our lunch. In the meantime, show me your wares."

Isabelle leaned across her swollen tummy to reach a shopping bag, then smiled self-consciously. "Baby's due next week, but it feels like he's about to pop out any minute."

"A boy?"

"Yes, he'll be Brian Lee or Brian Lee Levy, if he doesn't look too Asian. My husband says he'll have a hard time in school if he looks Chinese with a Jewish name."

So she was married and obviously, to a Caucasian.

Conversation halted temporarily while Cas rattled off an order and Hallie examined the four beaded purses Isabelle set on the table. They were not her taste, but they were handmade and unique, and her friends might like them. Feigning admiration and excitement, she wrote out a check for all four.

Cas watched the procedure with detached amusement. When their business was done, he turned to Isabelle. "I've a confession to make. We had an ulterior motive inviting you to lunch today."

"Oh?"

"Remember telling me you wanted to do something for Dale Redington?"

"Yes, certainly. Did you ask him what I could get for him?"

"No, but Hal and I have an idea." The waiter set down a platter of prawns with black bean sauce, string beans with tofu and a bowl of brown rice. "I'll serve the food and let my equal half take over the story."

Hallie launched into an abridged version of what led up to their lunch, stressing how anxious Dale was to find the mother of the abandoned baby.

"Jenna's notes mentioned a lawyer who specializes in adoptions," Hallie explained. "I'd like to see this man and if you were to come with me, we could ask questions about pregnant women who don't want their babies. He could be the key to finding Jenna."

"Impossible!" Isabelle clasped her stomach protectively. "I would never tell anyone I'm going to give up my baby!"

"No, no, this would just be a meeting to get information. We wouldn't lie about anything, we'd just ask questions. And attorney-client privilege guarantees our conversation would be confidential."

"I'm sorry, but I don't think I could do that."

"You don't have to decide now," soothed Cas. "Go home, think it over, remember that this would mean a great deal to Dale — more than any gift you could buy him. And it would only take about an hour of your time."

"He's right," added Hallie. "If you're nervous or uncomfortable, we understand. But do sleep on it and call me in a day or so. Right now, lunch looks yummy, so let's dig in."

Early that evening, Isabelle called. She was having contractions and they were off to the hospital.

— Chapter 59 —
May-June, 2009

THE NEWS OF BRIAN LEE LEVY'S entrance into the world (nine pounds, fifty-four centimeters) came to Hallie via email. She ordered a baby gift online and received a warm note in return. The P.S. indicated that now that her son was born and duly registered, Isabelle would be happy to pay a visit to the lawyer.

Hallie lost no time calling for a "No-Obligation Free Consultation," and made an appointment for the first Thursday in June.

Cyril J. Greenberg, Esq. practiced law in an impressive eighteenth floor office in the Financial District, not far from the Golden Gate Star. The building was old San Francisco, formerly a bank, and the furnishings were dark wood to match the moldings.

Hallie and Isabelle approached a desk where a blonde in horn rims looked up pleasantly. "Miss Marsh?"

"Yes and this is Ms. Lee. We have a ten o'clock appointment."

"Please have a seat. We'll be right with you."

"Lawyers always make you wait," Hallie whispered to Isabelle. "They want you to know how busy they are."

No sooner had they sat down, however, than a side door opened and an older, slightly overweight woman appeared. Her hair was straight and short, her pantsuit mannish, her body language formidable. *"Don't-screw-with-me,"* said her every movement. She beckoned with an outstretched arm.

"Hello," said Hallie, as they approached. "We have an appointment with Mr. Greenfield."

"I'm Cyril Greenfield," she said. "Will I do?"

"Oops!" Hallie grinned and offered a hand. "I'm *so* sorry! I don't know why I…"

"Not to worry, it happens all the time. You're Ms. Marsh and Ms. Lee? Come in, have a chair."

As soon as they were seated, the lawyer spoke. "You mentioned you're interested in the process of adoption." She looked at Isabelle. "Forgive my directness, but are you pregnant?"

Isabelle nodded. "No. I had a baby a month ago."

"Congratulations. How may I help you?"

Hallie interceded. "We just want information."

"I understand. Let me assure you that everything said in this office is confidential and you are no obligation whatsoever. Our usual process is to work with the birthmother during her pregnancy. We match her with the right adoptive parents — they're carefully interviewed, their home is investigated, and if they're approved, they pay all her expenses — medical, housing, legal — until the baby is born."

"And if the baby's already born?" asked Hallie.

"Same thing. The adoptive parents pay legal and all expenses relating to the adoption. But before we get into any details, I'm going to give both of you a kit with a CD and all the information you'll need. The first page of the booklet is important. It tells how our firm began, twenty-four years ago."

"Were you the founder?" ventured Isabelle.

"Yes. I'm proud of our reputation for honesty and integrity, as you'll see from the letters on the wall, including one from Senator Feinstein. We've received many awards and honors over the years."

"Impressive," murmured Hallie.

The attorney handed each woman a large envelope, then looked directly at Isabelle's left hand. "I see you're married."

"Um — yes."

"And I assume your husband doesn't want you to give up the baby?"

"Well, um, yes. I mean no. I mean —"

With a loud sigh, the attorney folded her arms and frowned. "I think we've danced around long enough. Suppose you two ladies stop playing me and tell me who you are and why the hell you're taking up my time."

Momentarily stunned, Hallie recovered quickly.

"You're absolutely right, Ms. Greenfield, and I apologize for confusing you. We are who we say we are and we're here for information. I asked Isabelle to come along because I was afraid you wouldn't see us if I told you the real reason."

"Go on."

"It has to do with a man who worked for you — Shane Snow."

"Shane? He died last year."

"I know. Since then, his wife has disappeared under strange circumstances. My fiancé, Dan Casserly —"

"The writer?"

"Yes."

"I've read his books. I'm a big fan. Is this a story he's investigating?"

"Yes, but not to write about it." Hallie took a few minutes to fill in some background, never mentioning Vicky. Then she summed up, "All we really want from you, Ms. Greenfield, is some information on Shane, and his job of procuring babies. We're hoping the facts we gather will lead us to Jenna."

"Call me Cyril. You should've been straight with me, Ms. Marsh. And I applaud Ms. Lee for not being able to lie. But you've got me curious. I'm sorry to hear about Shane's wife. I met her a few times and I liked her. She had passion for her causes."

"Black market babies was one of them."

"She mentioned that and said she wanted to talk to me. I wondered why I never heard from her. But what goes on under the radar is not my bailiwick. We believe in

167

private legal adoption, which is more ethical and more personal than agency adoption."

"Why is that?"

"They have the reputation of high-pressuring young women and not caring about their feelings. You probably know I had to fire Shane just before he went fishing."

"No, I didn't know."

"I asked questions and I didn't like his answers. Then I found out he was getting signed relinquishments from mothers by threats and coercion. Today, so many young girls get pregnant and don't want their parents to know. They get someone like Shane to 'sponsor' them — that means he gets them into the hospital under a false name, falsifies the birth record and tells the mothers their baby died."

"How awful!"

"That's only the tip of the glacier. Brokering babies has become a $1.4 billion dollar industry."

"No wonder Jenna was so concerned. Isn't it possible that Shane simply tried to persuade these girls?"

"Persuasion is illegal and immoral. It's not the way we work. I happen to be strongly pro-choice. Unlike most adoption agencies, we don't vilify abortion clinics. If a woman doesn't want to carry a pregnancy to term, go through labor, then never see the child again, in my book, she's welcome to have an abortion."

"And," she went on, "so many of these 'pro-life' teenagers who keep their children have no money and end up on Welfare. It costs the average parent $222,000 to raise a child to the age of seventeen today. Kids have to have cell phones, computers, you-name it."

"Then how do you find babies?"

"We spend millions advertising on the Internet. We market to schools, social workers, church groups, physicians, hospitals, medical clinics, teenager programs, you-name-it. We're aggressive, but not persuasive. That's an important distinction and Shane ignored it. I've learned that he was even importing babies from other countries."

"Wow!"

"He was also selling babies to couples who wanted to adopt, but didn't want to go through the long, legal process. These would-be parents wouldn't have passed the screening process, the in-depth interviews and investigations, much less pay the birthmother's expenses."

Hallie felt her heart quicken. "Do you know of an actual case where Shane bought or sold a black market baby? Could you give me an example?"

"No, I haven't time. But I will have my assistant make copies of everything in Shane's file that isn't confidential. I'm not sorry the SOB's dead. He should've been strung up by his gonads. We'll mail you the papers in a day or so. Read them, come back, we'll talk. Bring Dan Casserly. I'd like to meet him. Now," she added, "Get the hell out of here."

— Chapter 60 —

THAT EVENING, Hallie couldn't wait to tell Cas that they would've been thrown out of the lawyer's office a lot sooner had she not mentioned his name. "Cyril's a big fan of yours. She told me so."

Cas rolled his eyes. "And you believed her? Remember the old joke about how you know when lawyers are lying?"

"Yeah, when their lips move. That's older than I am."

"Maybe so, but lawyers aren't exactly known for their honesty. She had no right to bawl you out. You were just being creative."

"I never was a good actor. But I feel we're on the right track. I'm convinced Cyril is a woman of integrity and had no part of what Shane was up to."

A week later, mid-morning, FedEx delivered Shane's papers in a wooden box. Hallie was amazed to learn that he'd spent twelve years working for Cyril. During that time, he claimed to have found more than two hundred adoptable babies —a remarkable record.

The birthmothers' contact info was inked out in the files, but the new parents were named, along with the date of their "acquisition," their home, email addresses and phone numbers.

One couple, who'd adopted their son ten years ago, lived in Pacific Heights, not far from Hallie's apartment. She tried their phone number and a woman with a pleasant voice answered.

She turned out to be Daphne Peterson, mother of ten-year-old Jake Peterson, who was, at the moment, in school. Hallie explained that she was investigating the disappearance of Shane Snow's wife and that they were talking to people who had worked with Shane. Did she remember him?

Indeed she did. He'd helped arrange the adoption and had been very caring.

The woman explained that her son, Jake, knew he'd been "specially chosen" and was comfortable with the knowledge, as well as being a bright, popular child. The adoption, however, was not "open." That meant that the sixteen-year-old birthmother had signed away her rights. She wanted no further connection with her baby. The father, they'd been told, was an unknown teenager.

Although Daphne Peterson didn't see how she could be of help, she invited Hallie for tea that afternoon.

The young mother was friendly and gracious, and Hallie felt comfortable chatting in her living room. They were soon on a first name basis, and Hallie (with her usual economy of words) lost no time asking, "How did you meet Shane Snow?"

"We'd been trying to get pregnant for a few years," Daphne answered, clasping her hands in her lap. "We'd spent a fortune on fertility doctors, with no luck. Then a girlfriend happened to mention a Baby Fair in Sausalito. It was mainly for people with babies, but I was curious, so I decided to go with her."

"This was ten years ago?"

"More like eleven. And what a scene! Vendors were peddling everything from pre-heated diapers to cell phones for three-year-olds! One section offered services — nannies, baby sitters, Lamaze classes, photographers, even adoption.

Shane Snow was manning that booth and while my friend was off negotiating crib blankets, Shane — in a nice, non-pushy way — began telling me about what they did."

"Sounds like he charmed you."

"He was convincing. He called himself an 'Adoption Consultant' and said he would guide us through the whole process. Harvey and I hadn't given up trying to get pregnant and hadn't seriously considered adoption, but when he told me about this sad little pregnant teenager who was going to have to give up her baby boy — he made me feel as if I had to save that child."

"Did you ever think about having a surrogate?"

"Yes, we talked with Shane about it. He told us that fifty percent of mothers who offer their babies for adoption, including surrogates, change their minds. But he knew this young mother had no other options."

"Was Shane against abortion?"

"Strongly! When I told him we were horrified at the notion of killing babies, he agreed vehemently. Said that was why he got into the adoption business. Why do you ask?"

"It seems logical. When was the baby due?"

"In a month. Shane said we'd have to pay some expenses, including the mother's hospitalization. We were stunned when we learned the amount, but how can you put a price on a child?"

"Hope you don't mind my asking — five figures?"

"Six, I'm afraid — and then some."

If Hallie had had any doubts that Shane Snow was of questionable character, they melted away. But she simply said, "I'm sure it was money well spent."

After the better half of an hour, Jake Peterson, a lively, energetic youngster, came home from school, hugged his mother, shook hands with her guest and headed for the kitchen.

Hallie thanked Daphne warmly and they spoke of getting together for lunch. But as soon as she got to her car, she grabbed her iPhone and sent Cas a message: "You won't believe what I'm going to tell you!"

— **Chapter 61** —

THE SOUND OF the front door opening set Hallie's heart beating. She waited a few moments for Cas to shed his jacket and briefcase, then ran to meet him.

"I told you I was interviewing that woman with an adopted son?" she said breathlessly. "Well, guess what? I met the son."

"And?"

"And he's the spittin' image of Shane Snow!"

Cas laughed and pulled her to him. "Your imagination's running wild. What have you thawed for dinner?"

"Stuffed peppers. Stouffer's." She pulled gently away. "Remember that wedding picture of Shane? He's got a nice smile and a small space between his two front teeth. Jake Peterson has that same tooth gap. It's genetic. I'll bet anything he's Shane's son."

"Shouldn't be too hard to prove. I've got Shane's toothbrush for his DNA. Can you get the boy's?"

"I guess I could. But I've been thinking it over. It

would devastate that family if the truth were known. They'd never feel the same about Jake and the kid would be totally traumatized. I mean — what happened? Did Shane rape the mother? Did he impregnate her purposely?"

"Hold on, you're going too fast. Let's talk and eat. Better yet, let's eat and talk." Cas led the way to the kitchen. "Won't you sit down and join me in the dinner you didn't cook?"

"How can you eat at a time like this?" Exasperated, Hallie reached in the microwave and slapped down two steaming hot peppers. "This could be a major news story! What if Shane fathered *all* those babies he supposedly found?"

"Unlikely. Besides, you just said if Shane really was Jake's father, you didn't want the Petersons to know."

"I don't want them to know."

"Then let's not rush to conclusions. The first thing you have to do is check out some of Shane's other adoptions. Bring the kids gooey chocolate and collect napkins with their DNA."

"Good idea. I have two appointments with mothers around the time school gets out. If you give me Shane's toothbrush, I'll take everything to the DNA lab."

"I'll get it for you after dinner," he said, attacking his pepper.

"By the way, I checked the Physicians Desk Reference for those yellow capsules you found in Shane's bathroom. They're Nembutal Sodium or pentobarbital, a strong central nervous system depressant and sedative. He probably bought them from a dealer."

"Fine. Do you want a stuffed pepper?"

"No, thanks. They're both for you."

"I hoped you'd say that. Well, I've done some research, too. Remember my telling you I found Shane's million dollar life insurance policy?"

"Sure. You said he left half to his brother Finnegan and half to Jenna."

"Right." Cas set down his fork. "And if either heir died or was unable to claim it within six months of Shane's death, the other would get the full amount. I called the company. They weren't anxious to talk, but I did learn that Finnegan Snow collected $500,000 and they're trying to find Jenna to give her the rest."

"Interesting."

"There's more. Finnegan went to court to collect Jenna's half, but the judge said there was insufficient evidence that she was dead, and gave the insurance company two years to try to find her. If they can't, or if she doesn't show up by November, it all goes to — guess who?"

"Duh – Finnegan?"

"Bingo! So with Shane dead, he had a strong motive to get rid of Jenna."

"Murder?" she asked.

"People have gotten killed for a lot less. What do we know about Finnegan Snow?"

"Not much, although Jenna's notes indicate the brothers were close. She refers to him and Shane as 'best friends.' Speaking of friends, could I call your old girlfriend at the police station and see if either brother has a record?"

"Sure, just ask for Helen Kaiser. Last I heard she was

promoted to Sergeant." Cas reached for her hand. "You know, you're getting to be a darn good investigator."

"Thanks," she smiled. "Nothing like praise from Caesar."

PART 10

— Chapter 62 —

mid-June, 2009

ACROSS THE CITY, in his office at St. Paul's Hospital, Dr. Mitchell Cummings picked up the phone and dialed the physical therapy center. "Sara Bowman, please."

"She's with a patient," came the reply. "May I take a message?"

"Who is this — Jennifer? Anette?"

"Genelle."

Wouldn't you know he'd get the oldest nurse in the hospital. "It's Dr. Cummings, Genelle. Would you please find Sara and send her to my office?"

"As soon as she's through, I'll give her the message."

"Thanks," he snapped and hung up.

The physical therapy center was at its busiest when Genelle found Sara buckling a patient's legs to one of the Pilates machines.

"Dr. Cummings wants to see you in his office," she whispered.

Sara looked up irritably. "Did you tell him I was with a patient?"

"Yes. I said you'd go when you're through."

"Thank you, Genelle." Sara forced a smile. "I didn't mean to growl at you. It's just that his sense of timing isn't the greatest."

"Tell me about it." The nurse knew almost everything that went on in the hospital. Little escaped her.

Twenty minutes later, Sara found the surgeon seated at his desk, staring at his computer. He no longer stood when she entered.

"Hello, Mitch. You wanted to see me?"

"Yes," he said, "Thanks for coming. I know you're busy, but we haven't talked in a while. Please sit down."

The politeness was a thin veneer. Something was amiss. She took a chair and waited.

"It's been over a month since Dale left for that clinic," he began. "He was supposed to stay in touch and let me know what was going on. I haven't heard a word. And he *is* still my patient."

Was, she thought, but said nothing.

"I was told he was going for a week or two, for some rehab. But I'm starting to think he must like the place. What have you heard from him and don't lie to me."

"I have no intention of lying to you."

"Good. Because I saw the way he looked at you when they took the bandages off his eyes. The man's in love with you."

"If he is, he's never told me about it."

"You're going to tell me you haven't heard from him?"

"No, I've heard from him. And he does like the clinic. He thinks it's a bit overblown and he doesn't go for all the fancy therapies, but he found a Zen Garden where he can meditate, and he met a nice friend."

"Female?"

"Male."

"What about the doctors? The treatments? What does he say about me?"

"He hasn't mentioned you, at least, not to me. He likes Dr. Cossa, says he's brusque, but thorough."

"Damn!" Mitch banged his fist on the desk. "Why didn't I see this coming?"

"See what?"

"We could lose him and the whole Redington family, that's what. If he develops an attachment to Dr. Cossa and that — that place — he could transfer all his loyalty to them!"

"I don't think he thinks about things like that, Mitch. He knows what wonderful work you did for him." And he also knows you're screwing his wife, she thought.

"I should never have encouraged him to go." He scratched his forehead. "Time for damage control. We've got to get him out of that place and back home before it's too late. I need your help."

"Talk to Daisy."

"Daisy doesn't have any influence. But you do. He'd do anything you asked."

Sara tried for control. She mustn't lose her temper.

"Do you have his phone number?" he continued. "If not we can get it. We have to have some excuse. Maybe we could say I was looking at his x-rays and saw something suspicious. Something we have to tend to right away."

"If you want to tell him a lie, you call him."

"You're the one he cares about. Do you have a better idea?"

"No."

"Well, think about it! If we lose Dale, we lose our whole future. My new clinic goes down the drain and your high-paying job with it. We can't let that happen!"

It was time to speak up. "I don't have a job with

your new clinic, Mitch. And what you're talking about is beyond unethical. From what little I know, Dale is happy at Cossa. He's finding peace of mind and he's beginning to heal emotionally. Here — there's his family and a thousand distractions. We would be medically and morally culpable if we were to scare him into coming home now."

The doctor seemed shaken. "Do you not understand what's at stake?"

"I do understand."

"And you're not willing to try to save your future?"

"I'm not willing to do what you ask."

"Don't you care about your job?"

"Is that an ultimatum?"

"Call it what you want. Take a day to think it over."

"I don't need a day. I won't be a party to lies and deception."

"Oh, cut the shit, Sara. You're no angel."

She rose. "I'm done, Mitch."

"You're fired," he said.

— Chapter 63 —

NO SOONER had Sara left his office, than Mitch sent word that she was to gather her possessions, leave the hospital immediately and not return. Her friends on the staff were shocked and angry, and when told what happened, were even angrier.

"He can't fire you," protested Genelle. "He doesn't have the power."

"He has the power to make my life miserable," Sara

answered. "I can't possibly work with him."

Tears streamed down the nurse's face as she helped Sara empty her locker, and promised to let the patients know where to reach her.

That evening, after chatting with her brother Roger, Sara began to feel a new sense of freedom. Roger had urged her to report Mitch, but she knew he was already in for trouble. One of the nurses was quietly gathering signatures for a sexual harassment suit.

Sara reassured Roger that Mitch wouldn't dare blacken her record; she knew too much about him.

Her situation, in fact, was neither surprising nor distressing; she'd been thinking about leaving St. Paul's for months. The idea of moving back to Seattle crossed her mind briefly, but her heart was here, with Dale. And although he was too honorable to profess his feelings at this time, she had no doubt of them. Whether he would act on them or try to save his marriage…was uncertain.

Dale's call came at eight that evening and Sara quickly told the day's events. His first response was irritation that she'd been fired, but he also hoped he'd be able to see more of her. Then he asked if she had enough money to live on. She did.

Mitch's desperation to get funds for his clinic no longer surprised Dale. But nothing the man could say or do would stop him from having his scar surgery, scheduled for the following week. Dr. Cossa had said that if all went well, Dale could go home in ten days. A surgeon he knew in the Bay Area could do the follow-up.

"Just be on guard," were Sara's last words. "Mitch has the morals of a maggot."

— Chapter 64 —

THE SUN WAS HIGH in the sky the next morning when an attendant found Dale at his usual seat in the Tea Garden. "There's a call for you, sir. It's from your son. He says it's important."

"Jimmy?" Dale jumped up, set his book on the table and followed the man to the phone. "Jimbo, are you there?"

"Sorry to disturb you, Dad. But you better come home. Mom's in bad shape."

"What's wrong with her?"

"Mitch doesn't know. He thinks maybe it's some kind of food poisoning or maybe somethin' worse. She sees funny things that aren't there. She says she feels like shit and she pukes a lot."

"Has she seen Hadley, her primary doctor?"

"I dunno. It just started today. D'ya think you can come home?"

"I'd like to, but I've got surgery coming up. Tell you what. I'll call Hadley Harris and ask him to stop by and see Mom. Don't tell Mitch about Hadley — doctors get their feathers ruffled easily. Just tell Mitch you spoke to me and I'll be home as soon as I can."

"Don't you care about Mom?"

"Of course I care and if Hadley says I'm needed, I'll be on the next plane. But I'm not too worried about food poisoning. You feel miserable and think you're going to die for a few days, then it all goes away. Do we have a deal?"

"Yeah. D'ya think Mitch'll be pissed?"

"Mitch is a plastic and reconstructive surgeon and should not be treating your Mom for this. Stay cool, keep your cell phone on and I'll call you as soon as I hear back from Hadley."

"Okay, Dad. I really miss you."

"Me, too, Jimbo. Me, too."

— Chapter 65 —

DALE WAS WORRIED. Would Mitch really stoop to making Daisy sick just to get him home? He left an urgent message for Hadley Harris. When the physician finally called, Dale told him exactly what was going on and why, and asked him to check up on Daisy.

He did so and reported back: "I don't have a diagnosis yet. She has mydriasis — dilated pupils, a fever, flushed skin and occasional hallucinations. I don't know what drugs or medication, if any, Mitch gave her. There was no sign of pills."

"Can you pump her stomach?"

"Not a good idea. We could perforate her intestines."

"Is she in pain?"

"No, she's sedated and sleeping. I called an ambulance and brought her here to the hospital for tests. We've taken blood and urine for a tox screen. We'll know more in an hour or so."

"For God's sake, Hadley, don't let Mitch get near

her! I don't put anything past him, not even poisoning her."

"That's taken care of. Her room is isolated."

"Thanks, Doc, and please call me back, no matter how late."

The clock by his bed said ten-twenty when the phone finally rang. Hadley first reassured Dale that Daisy would recover. "The tox screen ruled out most common drugs, so it wasn't an overdose of anything," he said. "That was encouraging. I knew Daisy's symptoms were familiar, particularly the dilated pupils, the reddish skin and the delirium, but I couldn't put it all together. Then I went through my files and came across the case of two teenage boys I treated a few months ago. They had the same symptoms."

"And they survived?"

"Absolutely. When they recovered, I learned they'd been chewing the seeds of a common plant, *Datura stramonium*, better known as jimson weed. They'd heard it was hallucinogenic. It can also be quite toxic."

"You think Daisy —"

"Her symptoms are milder than what the boys had. And we don't have a lab test to prove it's Jimson. But the plant's main ingredients are the belladonna alkaloids atropine and scopolamine. The dilated pupils give it away."

"Where would she get something like that? She hates drugs. She wouldn't chew a bunch of seeds..."

"I don't know. It's a weed that grows wild and somehow found its way into Daisy's system. We've been giving her intravenous lorazepam and she's responding well.

185

She may be able to go home tomorrow."

"That's great news, Hadley. What can I do to thank you?"

"Take care of yourself, Dale. Daisy's going to be fine."

— Chapter 66 —
Two weeks later, July 1, 2009

SARA WAS TOO EXCITED to do anymore job scouting. After days spent visiting physical therapy and sports medicine centers in the major hospitals, as well as various independent clinics, she was feeling discouraged. Nothing had impressed her. Fortunately, she'd saved enough money to take some time off.

But the hours dragged until four that afternoon, when Dale's plane was due to arrive home. Daisy, of course, would pick him up at the airport. He'd promised to call Sara the first chance he got. She waited — and worried.

Dale was exhilarated. Imagine! — getting off the plane with no cane, no walker, just his own pair of feet. Those last two weeks at Eliva had been the best of his whole stay. The physical therapist who'd worked so hard with Dale's right arm, had even pronounced him "able to encircle a lovely lady."

The psychiatrist, sad to see him go, warned that he might have flashbacks and gave him pills to help if he did.

Patients in his support group were eager to exchange cards and email addresses, and his new confidant made him promise to visit Paris with the beautiful redhead he kept talking about.

Best of all, perhaps, was that Dr. Cossa, finally convinced that Dale was ready for surgery, had operated with amazing success. The scars were barely visible, the soreness minimal, and the big clunky bandage…only a memory.

Spotting their butler holding up a sign with his name, Dale followed him to the black limo. Waiting in the back seat, Daisy greeted him warmly.

On the advice of his lawyer, whom he'd talked to just before leaving Eliva, Dale tried to return her show of affection. But all he could think of was that he'd been told not to see or email Sara, or call her on the landline phones, which were probably tapped. Even a wireless call could be traced and used against him in a divorce court.

According to his attorney, who'd done some investigating, Dr. Mitchell Cummings was not above having Dale tailed, or even hiring someone to search his garbage. The lawyer's last warning was, "Don't tell Daisy you want a divorce just yet."

Much to Dale's surprise, however, Daisy had held his hand driving home from the airport, told him how much she loved him, but felt that the separation had been good for them and that perhaps they needed more time apart. Pretending to be crushed, Dale had offered to move out as soon as he could find a place.

Telling his son was hard, and Jimmy shed a few tears, then confessed he'd been expecting that news for a long time. He also told his Dad that he'd fallen in love and lost his virginity. Dale congratulated him, they laughed and hugged and Jimmy rode off on his bicycle to let his new girlfriend console him.

Daisy had stayed home long enough to have dinner with her husband, exuded love and caring, then left for people and places unknown. As soon as Dale heard the limo take off, he phoned Birdy, told her he was back and wanted to drop by and say hello.

— Chapter 67 —

TWENTY MINUTES LATER, Dale greeted his former nanny with double-cheek kisses and a warm embrace. Birdy stared at him wide-eyed. "I don't believe it!" she exclaimed, "You're just as handsome as you always were. Are you sure you didn't make up all that stuff about getting burned?"

"Pretty good story, huh?" He grinned. "I forgot you never saw me playing Scarface. Dr. Cossa's a bloomin' genius! My cheek's still swollen, but he says the red will fade and take the last of the scars with it."

She linked her arm in his as they strolled down the hall. "Are you home for good now? Was Daisy glad to see you?"

"She was thrilled. Told me how much she loved me, then asked for a separation. I'll be moving out soon."

"Really?" Birdy's face lit up. "Hallelujah! What took you so long?"

"Laziness and procrastination." He laughed. "I can tell I'm not going to get any sympathy here. Vicky asleep?"

"Yes." She opened the door so he could see her

crib. "Take a peek."

"She's beautiful!" He stared for a long moment. "You're doing a wonderful job, Birdy. I know Hallie and Cas will have some answers for us before long. If Jenna's alive, I promise you we'll find her."

"I pray for Jenna every day. I'll hate to lose Vicky, but she needs her mother."

"And I need your phone so I can talk to Sara — without my wife, her damn butler and God-knows-who-else listening."

"Aha! I suspected something was going on there. Sara would be perfect -"

"Your phone?"

"In the bedroom." Birdy pointed down the hall. "And close the door, please. I don't want to blush."

— Chapter 68 —

SARA ANSWERED on the first ring. "Hello?"

"Hi, darling," Dale said without thinking. "Uh — sorry. Anyway, I'm back, I'm rested, my scars are almost gone and life is starting to look rosy again. What about you?"

"I've been waiting for your call. Are your scars really gone?"

"You'll be amazed. Dr. Cossa's a miracle worker. I saw some of the other patients, before and after their surgeries. They look like new people. I can't thank you enough for finding him."

"I'm thrilled to hear it. How's Daisy?"

"Same as always. But I finally got the truth about her recent 'illness.' She told me Mitch said it was crucial that I come home before Dr. Cossa operated on my face. He said that if the Doc did a good job, I'd transfer my loyalties and that would be the end of his dream clinic. Thank goodness you warned me."

"Mitch is desperate. He'll do anything."

"Apparently so. Daisy said he gave her a cup of tea with some herb in it that would supposedly give her a slight fever for twenty-four hours, then she'd be fine. He neglected to mention she'd have delirium, vomiting and hallucinations."

"Classic Mitch. He poisoned her to get you to come home."

"Yup. And she said she agreed to go along with the plot because she missed me so much. Sure."

Sara worded her reply carefully. "Possibly there's more to it?"

"You and I both know they've been — what's Jimmy's word? — 'hooking up' for months! The bastard even had the guts to scare poor Jimmy into calling and telling me how ill his mother was."

"Wasn't Daisy angry that he made her so sick?"

"Mitch must have sweet-talked her out of it. But the hell with him. I've got some great news!" He didn't wait for a comment. "Daisy loves me so much she's kicking me out of the house. Tomorrow I look for a place."

"Honestly? You're separating?"

"We're divorcing. But she doesn't know that I know about her and Mitch. They both think I'm an idiot."

Sara burst into laughter. "Well, I think you're the most wonderful idiot on the planet. Golly, I hope I didn't cause —"

"You didn't cause anything. Daisy and I have been unhappy for years. The problem is, right now I'm at Birdy's. My lawyer won't let me see or call you again till we get things settled. We don't want you involved in the divorce."

"I understand," she said softly. "However long it takes — you're worth waiting for."

PART 8

— Chapter 69 —

August 3rd, 2009

MUCH TO DALE'S surprise and pleasure, his energy was fast returning, and the challenge of finding a new place to live excited him. He would have liked to buy a house for himself and Sara, but he was, after all, a married man.

It took him almost a month to find and rent a furnished South of Market penthouse, with two bedroom suites — one for Jimmy — and a roof deck. The panoramic view took in the Bay Bridge, a magical necklace of lights after dark.

On the first Monday in August, having given most of his books and "treasures" to the Salvation Army and having ascertained that Daisy was at the beauty salon, he took out a duplicate of her key, which he'd had the foresight to make, and once again opened her locked drawer.

The stack of letters had grown larger in his absence, and he quickly copied the most recent ones and returned them to their place. He would read them later.

When Daisy came home newly coiffed, manicured and pedicured, he grabbed the last of his clothes and toiletries, tucked his briefcase under his arm and kissed her cheek goodbye.

Daisy wore a long face and pretended he'd be coming back. They both knew otherwise.

The first call Dale made from his new sitting room was to Cas and Hallie, who were pleased that he was home from Eliva, and accepted his invitation to stop by the next evening and catch him up on their search.

Though he'd never met either of them, Dale greeted his guests with hugs and champagne. After showing off his view and getting them seated, he asked, "Any news about Jenna?"

"I'm afraid it's not good," said Cas, "but we'll start where we left off."

He described how he and Hallie had studied Jenna's papers, how he happened to meet Isabelle Lee and learned of her desire to thank Dale for trying to save her grandfather.

"Isabelle had just had a baby," explained Hallie, "and because we said it would be doing a favor for *you*, she agreed to go with me to see Cyril J. Greenfield, the female lawyer who employed Shane Snow. Cyril quickly realized that Isabelle wasn't giving up her baby for adoption."

"But Isabelle tried to help," said Dale. "I'd like to thank her."

"I'll give you her number. She did get us in the door. Once Cyril realized the real reason we were there, she confirmed that Shane's job was to find babies for adoption. She said Shane had been evading questions and lying about his sources, so she had to fire him. When we told her Shane's wife Jenna had mysteriously disappeared, she agreed to send me Shane's work notes — whatever wasn't confidential."

"She kept her word," Hallie went on, "I got his files. The names of the babies' mothers were blacked out, but the names of the adoptive parents were there. So I met some of them. One adopted boy looked a lot like Shane and we wondered if Shane acquired his babies by fathering them."

"Good Lord! Could you get their DNA?"

Hallie shook her head. "Not from Jake Peterson, the

boy who looked like him. But I did get DNA from the others and none matched Shane's. He may have fathered Jake Peterson, but if so, it only happened once that we know of. And we weren't about to ruin Jake's life. It was disappointing, but that lead, unfortunately — or maybe fortunately — went nowhere."

— Chapter 70 —

"WE'VE MADE progress, though," Cas explained, continuing the conversation with Dale. "Hallie called our police sergeant friend, Helen, who checked to see whether Shane or his brother, Finnegan Snow, had a record. Neither did. But that didn't stop our fearless investigator."

Hallie laughed. "I got lucky. I bought some Luminol online."

Dale squinted. "You bought what?"

"I guess you don't watch *Law and Order*. It's a chemical the police use to detect blood, even when it's been scrubbed clean. I sprayed Luminol on several rooms in Jenna's house with no luck. Then I tried her office, and sadly, I found blood stains on the wall. They'd been cleaned, too. That was the first real indication of foul play."

Dale's face fell.

"I'm terribly sorry," Hallie went on. "I called the police and they sent out a blood spatter analyst. He figured the angle of origin of the spatter and could tell me that Jenna was sitting at her desk. He said she must have suffered acute cerebral hemorrhaging — blunt force trauma — from a single blow to the back of her head. That was determined by what they call MVIS — Medium Velocity Impact Spatter."

"Sounds like high velocity to me," said Cas.

"No, high velocity would have been a gunshot wound or an explosion. The blood on the wall proved to be Jenna's, and contained tiny cement fragments. The officer guessed she was bludgeoned to death ten to twelve months ago. There was no chance she could have lost that much blood and survived. The only certainty was that she was murdered."

"Poor Jenna. Poor Vicky," moaned Dale.

"We haven't told anyone about Vicky," Cas assured him. "We're still checking to see if Jenna or Shane might have some family who can take her. So far, no luck."

"What about Shane's brother?"

"Finnegan Snow had a lot of money to gain from Jenna's death and could well be involved. So before we tell him about Vicky, we'd better make sure he's not our perp. We're going to try to solve the murder first."

"Aren't the police working on it?" asked Dale.

"They are, but they have other priorities."

"I do watch some TV," said Dale. "Isn't the husband always the first suspect?"

"Shane would be," Hallie answered. "But Jenna was alive *after* Shane died. Just to verify, I called the doctor at the hospital in Alaska who signed the death certificate. He remembered Finnegan Snow and how distressed he was about losing his brother. The doc said it was hospital policy to perform an autopsy when death occurs suddenly and the deceased was in apparent good health."

"Did they do one?"

"No. The Medical Examiner had a backlog of bodies and they weren't anxious to add another, especially a non-resident. So they ruled Shane's death 'unexpected' rather than suspicious. If Finnegan had wanted an autopsy, he'd have had to pay $2500, and he told the doctor he couldn't afford it. Cremation was the cheapest way to go."

"A last point," Hallie continued. "There was no blood anywhere else in the house. The spatter expert said the killer must have stuffed Jenna's body in a suitcase or a plastic bag and carried her out of the house — possibly down the back stairs to a car in the garage. What happened after that, no one knows."

Dale sighed. "Isn't it time we let the police take over and solve the case?"

"By all means," said Cas, "but I've a hunch Hallie will solve it first."

— Chapter 71 —

WORRIED ABOUT Vicky's future, Dale decided to hold off telling Birdy that Jenna was not coming back. He would pass along the sad news as soon as he had some answers. *Were* there any family members who might want the child? What role, if any, did Finnegan Snow play in Jenna's murder? An idea was taking shape in the back of his mind, and the next morning he went to see his lawyer.

Driving to One Maritime Plaza, a huge metallic building near the Embarcadero, Dale thought about Daisy's most recent letters from Mitch, and how they had angered and sickened him. Mitch was pushing hard for Daisy to get her divorce, and repeatedly urged her to take nothing less than a multi-million dollar settlement, which she'd already promised to invest in his clinic.

Inside the lawyer's office, the barrister and his client made plans. Dale would see Daisy that afternoon. "It's clear she wants a divorce," the attorney advised, "let her bring up the subject. Then tell her to have her lawyer call me. If we have to get nasty, you don't have to be involved."

"Above all," he'd added, "don't promise her anything — not alimony, not custody of Jimmy, not the house. I'll need those for bargaining power. And do not, under any circumstances, let her get to you with tears and pleas."

Later that day, Dale did talk to Daisy. She did suggest the "D" word, as she called it, and they agreed to have their lawyers work out details.

The explosion came a week later, sooner than expected. Once Dale's lawyer revealed he had copies of Mitch's love letters, there was no denying her infidelity. But it wasn't Daisy who phoned to plead with Dale, it was her frantic lover. Admitting he'd made a mistake falling for his "best friend's wife," Mitch insisted it was all Daisy's idea to get a big settlement and invest it in his clinic.

Lies followed more lies, Dale finally told him to perform an impossible anatomical function and hung up. The next day he changed his phone number. The battle had begun.

— Chapter 72 —

DALE'S DESIRE for a peaceful end to his marriage was running into obstacles. Mitch and Daisy were deep into fabrications and threats; Dale's lawyer, a seasoned veteran of the marital wars, held firm and strong. He enjoyed a good fight, particularly when he possessed "weapons of mass destruction," as he referred to the love letters.

He was even able to decipher the mysterious "BTL" which appeared at the end of each missive. At a meeting with Daisy and her lawyer, she'd blurted out that she'd promised Mitch she would "Burn This Letter" every time he sent one. Touched by their content, however, she hadn't been able to destroy them.

Failure to do so, Dale's lawyer reported, had significantly dampened Mitch's "love" for Daisy. The surgeon knew that his career, as well as his marriage, would be ruined if ever the letters became public. Yet despite his anger and frustration, he'd continued to court Daisy as if nothing had changed.

If the couple could settle quietly out of court, and if Daisy did get a multi-million dollar settlement, she might still have some value for him.

The end came sooner than expected. In a closed courtroom, a judge ruled that the letters could not be blocked as evidence.

The setback was an enormous blow to Daisy. The lawyers argued for another week, Daisy tried unsuccessfully to see or talk to Dale, then tearfully agreed to the terms.

She would get joint custody of Jimmy, their $14 million mansion, its expensive art and furnishings, their limo, plus $10,000 a month for ten years, whether she remarried or not. After that, the alimony would cease and her own significant investments would support her nicely. All Dale wanted from the house was his player piano.

On September 14th, 2009, the Redington marriage was over. The divorce was uncontested, legally binding and enforceable. There was no multi-million dollar settlement.

— Chapter 73 —
September, 2009

DALE COULDN'T WAIT to call Sara with the good news, remembering that his lawyer had warned him to wait at least a week before seeing her.

"Daisy's legal team will stoop to anything to keep her sending those fat checks," he'd said, "including having you followed. If they can show evidence that you and Sara were carrying on at the same time as Daisy and Mitch were, they could try to claim fraud and contest the divorce."

"But we *weren't* carrying on," Dale had protested. Nevertheless, he took the advice and told Sara that he'd take her to dinner in a week and explain everything.

His next call was to Hallie, in her office. He brought her up to date, accepted her congratulations, and asked if they'd had any luck finding Jenna's relatives.

"We've been hot on the trail of Finnegan," she said. "He's not listed anywhere, not even on Google. It seems he doesn't want to be found, except by the insurance company.

As you know, they paid him half a million from Shane's policy and they've been trying to find Jenna to give her the other half."

"Isn't there a time limit?"

"Yes, Shane had stipulated that if either Finnegan or Jenna was unable to receive the inheritance within six months from the date of his death, the survivor would get the rest. The insurance company took it to court and the judge upped the time limit to two years. That means that two months from now, in November, Finnegan expects to collect."

"Did the insurance company give you his address?"

"Reluctantly — after Cas convinced them they'd save a bundle if we could prove Finnegan killed Jenna. But we can't. Right now, he's just a suspect."

"What about Vicky — wouldn't she inherit Jenna's money?"

"You asked us not to involve Vicky and we haven't."

Dale was irate. "What are the cops doing?"

"Two men from the Sonoma Police Department went to talk to Finnegan, but they couldn't tie him to the crime. They couldn't even get a search warrant. Mr. Snow is very elusive."

"Where does he live?"

"He owns a vineyard in Glen Ellen, in Sonoma Valley. His girlfriend comes from a well-known wine family. She swore to the police that they were driving home from Las Vegas about the time Jenna disappeared. She claims she can't remember the name of their motel and has no proof."

Dale sighed. "Have you tried to find Jenna's body?"

"Yes — no luck with hospitals."

"Morgues?"

"We've tried them, too. They can keep a body indefinitely if it's related to an open police investigation, but even if they found Jenna's body, her killer would've made sure she had no ID. If no one claimed or identified her, she'd have gotten a 'pauper's burial.' And they can't exhume the body because they wouldn't know which body to exhume."

Dale looked thoughtful a few seconds, then he said, "What would you do if you wanted to dispose of a body?"

"I asked Cas that same question. He said he'd try to find a way to cremate it, just like Finnegan did with Shane's body."

"And hope to get away with murder — literally."

"Right. But we may be on to something. At least 40 funeral homes do cremations in the Bay Area, and while you were busy getting divorced, I've been visiting them with Jenna's picture. So far, nobody's recognized her, but one funeral director told me – in confidence — that the Kragen Crematory in Oakland gets a lot of bodies that have been mutilated in accidents or crimes. They have a reputation for not asking too many questions."

"You went there?"

"Sure. Mr. Kragen was very chatty. He told me he handled the incinerations ever since he lost his assistant. He went on and on about this man who'd worked for him for twenty-two years, won some money on a lottery ticket and quit in late August, last year."

Dale's eyes widened. "Maybe the assistant *didn't* win

a lottery. Maybe he got rid of Jenna's body — for a profit."

"It's a long shot, but possible. We know that on the morning of August 27th, 2008, Jenna asked Birdy to look after Vicky. Jenna said she'd be back in four days and went home to pack, but she never left the house — not alive, that is."

"Was she killed that day?"

"Had to be that afternoon or evening. The timing fits. The killer could have taken her body to be cremated the next day. Kragen, the owner, was home sick at the time and gave me the assistant's name and address. Cas has been traveling, but he's coming back Saturday and we're going to pay a call on Mr. Cal Ebsen."

"Good sleuthing," said Dale, "and good luck!"

— Chapter 74 —

CALVIN D. EBSEN lived a few blocks from Lake Temescal, in the northeastern hills section of Oakland. The forty-minute drive across the San Francisco Bay Bridge gave Hallie and Cas time to plan their approach.

After discarding a number of scenarios, they agreed to stick as close to the truth as possible. Cas would start the questions, then Hallie would join in.

They pulled up to a small house on a well-traveled street. Missing shingles and peeling paint contrasted with the well-kept homes on the block. The neighbors would not be friendly.

Hallie crossed her fingers in the air as Cas rang the bell. No one answered, so he pressed again. This time, a voice shouted, "Hold your shirt on, I'm coming!"

A minute later, the door swung open. An older man, probably in his seventies, rolled towards them in a wheelchair. A massive crop of white hair framed a pale, wrinkled face; the nose was bulbous, the eyes strained to see. The owner's hand was outstretched. "Been expecting you," were his first words.

Cas shook hands and introduced himself and Hallie as investigators working with the police. "Calvin Ebsen?"

"The one and only. Call me 'Eb.' Come in, come in." He wheeled himself into a room with a tattered couch and two wooden chairs. "Sit y'rselves down in my palatial mansion."

"Thank you." Hallie settled on the couch and gently asked, "You were expecting us?"

"Been waiting months. You're here about that girl's body, right?"

"We're not sure," said Cas, straddling a chair. "What was her name?"

"Jane friggin' Doe, for all I know. Someone bashed her head in." He scratched his eyebrow. "I didn't look too close, but I saw pieces of rock in her hair."

Hallie felt her heart race. "Did you cremate her?"

"Yup. That was my job — me'n Kragen, we worked together twenty-two years. People came in with bodies and went out with ashes."

"What makes you think we're here to arrest you?" asked Cas.

Eb grimaced. "Why else would you be here? The guy who brought her in was Mafia or something. He wore

204

this stupid cap and big dark goggles, like a pilot. He had no papers and he wouldn't sign nothing. I told him I didn't do illegal and he should take his effing corpse and go to hell. So what does he do? He takes out this wad of cash — all C-notes! He says, 'Twenty-five grand if you burn the stiff and don't ask no questions.' "

"Didn't you think that was — um, strange?"

"Yeah, Miss Hallie, damn right I did. The scumbag musta bumped her off himself. Why else would he be wavin' all that moola around?"

Cas reached into his briefcase for the picture of Shane and Finnegan. "Do you recognize the man?"

"Like I said, he was covered up. He had a beard like that guy on the right."

"Finnegan," murmured Cas. The room was silent as Eb continued, "I don't have no family. My wife went to heaven, bless her heart, about the time the docs found this bad lung tumor — mestastatic or something. I dumped thirty pounds, my muscles got so weak I couldn't walk, but I told Kragen I hadda keep working. I needed the dough for my mortgage, or I'd be out on the street."

"I'm so sorry," whispered Hallie.

"Oh hell, we all gotta go sometime. The docs gave me two — three years. I figured when things got bad, I'd head for the Golden Gate Bridge and pop in the ocean."

"I'm glad you didn't."

"Thanks, Miss. I didn't because the scumbag's cash paid the mortgage. I took it so I could croak at home. I told Kragen I'd won some bucks in the lottery."

"That was resourceful," said Hallie.

"You bet your butt, Miss." He frowned. "You're too pretty for a cop."

"We're not cops, Eb," Cas explained, "we're just trying to help them. And we're not here to arrest you. We're hoping you can lead us to that hoodlum. Do you remember anything unusual about the man or the body?"

Hallie dug into her purse for a picture. "Is this the young woman?"

Eb stared a long time. "Like I said, I didn't look close."

"But," she protested, "you do remember that she was young and that she had a bump —"

"It weren't no bump, Miss Hallie. Some scumbucket smashed her skull."

"I'm pretty sure it's the woman we're looking for. It's terribly important we find the man who did that, but we need some evidence. Do you remember the color of her hair? Her shoes? Was she wearing jeans?"

"Don't remember," he said. "I wasn't gonna tell the other thing, but I guess it don't matter now. I'll kick off before they can throw me in the jug."

Hallie leaned forward anxiously. "What other thing?"

He sighed. "Hey, nobody's perfect, right? Sometimes we lift stuff off the bodies."

"You do?" Hallie's voice jumped an octave. "Tell us you took something off that young woman's body. Please tell us, Eb, and we'll send you a case of wine. Two cases. Five cases!"

"Can't drink booze. Wait here." He whirled his

chair around and disappeared down the hall.

Hallie grabbed Cas's hand. "Dear God, if you're listening, please…"

"Don't get your hopes up, honey."

Minutes later, squeaky wheels announced Eb's return. He veered over to Hallie and handed her a frayed envelope. "I was gonna hock this, but it ain't worth spit. Found it under her shirt. The gangster guy musta missed it."

Breathless with anticipation, Hallie reached into the packet and drew out a thin, almost invisible chain. At the end was a heart-shaped silver locket. She opened it, gasped, and covered her mouth. Peering over her shoulder, Cas stared hard at the picture in the tiny frame, then looked upward and whispered, "There *is* a God."

The face belonged to Shane Snow.

— Chapter 75 —

DRIVING HOME after their meeting, Cas and Hallie were elated. Eb had agreed that if circumstances warranted and he lived long enough, he would testify against Finnegan. He couldn't pick him out of a line-up, but he could swear that a man of Finnegan's height and build had brought him a young woman's body and bribed him.

He could also swear that she'd had a badly smashed skull and that he, Eb, had "lifted" the woman's necklace before cremating her body.

"It *had* to be Finnegan," said Hallie, looking down at the silver heart Eb had sold her for a hundred dollars.

"With Eb's testimony and this locket, no one could doubt it was Jenna's body. And no one else had a motive."

"I'm not so sure," Cas replied. "What about that article she wrote? Two guys went to prison because of her story. And from her notes, she was about to expose the adoption underground. Maybe that lawyer —"

"No, Cyril J. Greenfield was very proud of her firm and her integrity. There's something else going on — something obvious that we're missing."

Cas shrugged. "I think it's time we told the police what we know. They'll want to pay another call on Mr. Finnegan Snow."

"Why don't *we* call on him?"

"Too risky, Hal. This is one desperate bastard with no scruples and a gun or three, I'm sure. Best we leave it to the police. I'll call Helen on Monday."

"Whatever you say, honey. You know best."

— Chapter 76 —
The Next Day, 2009

HALLIE WAS EXCITED. She hadn't the slightest intention of waiting till Monday. Sunday morning, she climbed out of bed early. Cas was still sleeping, and they'd agreed that she would go to her apartment to pay bills and tend to various matters, while he'd spend the day finishing a story.

Sara was buried in the Chronicle when Hallie strolled into the kitchen shortly after eight. "What's up with your hunk, Ms. Sara? Anything happening yet?"

"The divorce was only a week ago." Sara smiled.

"But we're having dinner tomorrow night."

"What are you wearing?"

"Does it matter?"

"Damn right it matters! Has to be a skirt, not pants. Do you have a pretty dress?"

"I thought I'd wear my black —"

"Black is for funerals. Blue is better. Powder blue. I have a dress you can wear. Men are suckers for pastels."

Sara laughed. "You're too much. Talk about a control freak!"

"A woman has to plan these things. Where are you going?"

"He told me to pick a restaurant. I love Italian food."

"French is better. Candlelight and wine. Soft music. Go for it! Now listen: Cas is busy writing today and I'm about to drive to Glen Ellen to see if I can get some answers to this Jenna situation. I'm very careful and I won't do anything reckless, but will you be here all morning?"

"Absolutely. I'm giving myself a facial."

"Good. If you don't hear from me by noon, would you please call Cas? Tell him I've gone to 440 Valley Vista in Glen Ellen."

"That sounds ominous. Hallie, you're not going to that awful man's house, are you?"

"Don't worry, silly. I know what I'm doing." With a quick wave, Hallie dashed down the hall, grabbed a blue dress from her closet, set it on Sara's bed, then disappeared out the front door.

— Chapter 77 —

SOME FIFTY minutes later, Hallie found herself on Arnold Drive in Glen Ellen, and relying on her GPS navigation system, headed for the hills. After cussing at the twisty turns and unmarked roads, she spotted a boy on a bicycle who was happy to direct her to Valley Vista.

Soon she was pulling up to what looked to be a small, unmarked house and vineyard. The numbers on the neighboring farm made her fairly sure she'd reached her destination. Just as she was parking on the street, a black convertible whizzed past her down the road. The top was closed, so all she could see was that the driver wore a cap and was female. It looked as if the car came from the house she was planning to visit.

At first glance, the Snow residence seemed a typical white clapboard farmhouse with a two-story frame under a triangular roof. Wooden steps led up to an open porch. As Hallie looked closer, she could make out a Chippendale-style bench and a pair of chairs. A manicured lawn added to the impression of a house tastefully decorated and well-cared-for.

Gathering pen and notebook, Hallie checked herself in the mirror, shed her San Francisco jacket for the Glen Ellen sunshine, and approached the front door. There was no bell, only a knocker. She rapped — lightly at first, then hard.

Quite suddenly, the door opened. A heavily-bearded man in a plaid shirt and dungarees greeted her pleasantly. "What can I do for you?"

He was taller than expected and better looking than his picture. "Mr. Finnegan Snow? My name's Hallie Marsh and I'm sorry to come unannounced, but I couldn't find your phone number."

"That's because we don't want it to be found." He eyed her closely. "What's this about?"

"My name's Hallie Marsh." She handed him a card. "I have a public relations firm in San Francisco, but that's not why I'm here. I've been working with the police to try to find your sister-in-law, Jenna Snow."

"Jenna?" He seemed surprised. "How did you get involved with this?"

"I knew Jenna when she worked at the Golden Gate Star. She needed stories and I needed publicity for my clients, so we helped each other. I called one day and was told she'd taken a leave and hadn't come back. No one seemed to know what happened to her, so I reported her missing."

"Well, come on inside," he said, opening the door wider. "Care for a cold drink?"

"No, thanks."

He peered down at her card. "Hallie?"

"Yes."

"How'd you get my address?"

"I mentioned I'm working with the police. But they've been so busy they haven't given this much attention. Would you mind answering a few questions? It won't take long, then I won't bother you any more."

"No, I don't mind." He led the way. "My girlfriend, Barbara, just remodeled our kitchen but it's not quite finished. Make yourself comfortable." He pointed to a chair, then opened the refrigerator. "Beer?"

"All yours," she smiled, sitting down beside a window. "Your home is lovely — and your vineyard is so much bigger than it looks from the front."

"I'm proud of our grapes and our certification. We do sustainable organic farming. No pesticides at all, just natural predators. But you didn't come to talk about that."

"No. I know you spoke to the Sonoma police, so forgive me if I ask the same questions, but when was the last time you saw Jenna?"

He popped open the bottle and took a swig. "Mmm, let's see — my brother Shane died on a fishing trip. Do you know about that?"

"Yes, I'd heard. I'm sorry for your loss."

"Thanks, it's been tough. We were close. The last time I saw Jenna was when I gave her Shane's ashes. She said something about scattering them at sea. She was going to call me about a Memorial Service, but I never heard from her."

"Do you have any idea where she might have gone?"

"How would I know? I thought she and Shane were a good couple, but she didn't seem too upset about his death. He was traveling most of the time. I've a hunch she may have met someone and took off with him. You hardly knew my sister-in-law. Why do you care?"

He was beginning to sound annoyed and she was getting nervous. "I was fond of her. The people she worked with feared foul play."

"Why would anyone want to hurt her?"

"She was working on some explosive stories. I remember hearing that Shane worked in adoption —"

His frown told her she had overstepped. "Hallie," he said, pulling up a chair beside her. "I think you know a lot more than you're telling me."

"It's just part of the investigation."

"And you drove all the way up here because you have nothing better to do?"

"No, I —"

He moved closer. "Who sent you?"

"No one – honestly! The police don't know, my fiancé doesn't know…"

"Fine. We'll have some time for me to get the truth out of you."

"I'm sorry, Mr. Snow," she said, rising. "This wasn't a good idea. I didn't mean to upset you."

"You're not going anywhere." He pushed her down on the seat. Reaching into a drawer, he grabbed a piece of rope. "Put your hands behind you."

"Oh, please! I didn't mean —"

"Do as you're told. I don't want to hurt you."

Reluctantly, she leaned forward and let him bind her wrists to the chair. The cord hurt and her fears were mounting fast. "I was fibbing, Mr. Snow. I did tell my fiancé that I was coming. He'll be here pretty soon."

"Quit lying." He reached on the floor for her purse and groped inside. "No weapons. Okay, I'll leave you here for an hour while I finish my pruning. When I come back, I expect answers. If you're lying again, I'll know it. I can get very persuasive."

"You can't leave me like this," she protested.

He burst into laughter. "Try me. And by the way, scream all you want. Barbara's gone shopping and the neighbors can't hear a thing."

Still chortling, he slugged down his beer, tossed the bottle in a can of garbage, and slammed the back door.

— Chapter 78 —

FEAR, AND THE REALIZATION that she'd blundered badly, clouded Hallie's mind, making it hard for her to concentrate. Yet she knew she had to think — to try to figure out how she could escape this madman and get to her car.

Thoughts, schemes, strategies paraded through her brain in rapid succession. They all came back to a single plan: first, she must free her hands.

After discarding a dozen possibilities, she began to stretch her legs, moving herself and her chair inch by inch towards the blue garbage can, one of three recycling containers in a row. The beer bottle lay atop a collection of newspapers, cans and jars, but reaching it seemed impossible.

Several tries later, she managed to kick over the blue container; its contents rolled out across the floor. The beer bottle lay a few feet beyond reach, and again, she inched her way towards it. Finally, she was able to grasp it between her shoes.

How to get the bottle from her feet to her hands was the next challenge. Desperate, but trying not to panic, she shifted all her weight to one side, managed to tip over her chair, and fell with it to the floor. Her head was safe, but her arm landed hard.

Ignoring the pain, she pulled herself and her chair through the garbage, released the bottle with her feet, then wiggled herself around to where she could grasp it with one hand.

No sooner had she done so, then, to her horror, the door opened. "What the hell?"

Snow hurried over. "You dumb bitch! You were going to break that bottle and try to cut your hands loose?"

Hallie nodded.

He sighed. "We get all sorts of wild animals. Any one of them could've knocked the can over. Barbara can sweep it up it later."

Grunting with displeasure, he lifted the chair and its occupant easily, and set them upright. Hallie sat quivering, trying not to show her terror.

"I'll say this for you," he said, eyeing her sharply. "You've got guts. Have you thought about what you want to tell me?"

She swallowed hard and spoke in a low voice. "I really don't know very much. My fiancé and I went over Jenna's papers. it looked like Jenna thought Shane was involved in something illegal. She was on the verge of writing about it. Maybe they fought about that before he went off fishing."

"Ah, that's good to know. The police know all that, too, no doubt."

"Yes, but they don't seem to care. I really don't care, either. It's time for me to mind my own business and get back to work. If you let me go now, I won't tell a soul what happened here. I promise!"

"Sorry, Hallie. You're quite pretty and ordinarily I'd have more personal plans for you, but time's a factor, so I have a gift instead." He reached in his pocket and brought out two yellow capsules she recognized immediately. They were Nembutal, the same strong sedative Cas had found in Shane's bathroom.

"These will relax you," he said. "Need water?"

She nodded a silent "Yes," a new scenario forming in her head as she reluctantly opened her mouth. He dropped the pills on her tongue, poured in some water, then closed her lips and watched her swallow.

"Now," he said, reaching for her purse, "All I need is your car keys."

— Chapter 79 —

WHEN SNOW returned to the kitchen an hour later, Hallie sat slumped in her chair. He quickly untied her wrists and slung her body over his shoulder. Outside, he carried her to her parked car, unlocked the door, placed her in the passenger seat, then ran around to the driver's side. Once seated, he held up her limp body with his right hand and started the motor with his left.

Several miles along a seemingly deserted street, he turned off at a heavily wooded spot. A long, narrow road, almost hidden in the trees, wound around to a rocky cliff leading down to a lake. After about ten minutes, he stopped the car and pulled Hallie over to the driver's seat. Placing her hands on the wheel, he jumped out, then reached in and pressed the accelerator.

As he watched the car move slowly down to the edge, the sound of laughing voices gave him a start. He couldn't afford to be seen, even by children. Crouching low, he made his way back to the highway where he'd left a truck earlier. With a quick glance back, he climbed in and sped off.

— Chapter 80 —

SARA WAS GETTING nervous. It was almost eleven and no word from Hallie. She called Cas, gave him the message and heard the alarm in his voice.

"Oh, God, Sara. Call police Sergeant Helen Kaiser right away. Tell her to send a Sonoma patrol car to that address. Tell her it's an extreme emergency, a woman's life is in danger! And tell the cops to hold on to Finnegan Snow until I get there. I'm on my way!"

"Will do."

Breaking all speed records, Cas arrived at the farmhouse in forty-nine minutes, grateful to see a police car parked in front. He tried the knob; the door opened. Tiptoeing inside, he followed the direction of voices and laughter to the kitchen, where he found Snow and two officers sitting around the center island.

Seeing Cas, the policemen jumped up. "Mr. Casserly?"

"Yes. What the hell's going on?"

"Detective Benson," said one, extending a hand. "We heard you wanted us to detain Finn — er, Mr. Snow. We've checked the house and grounds; everything's clear. There's no sign of a woman or a struggle."

"Except Finn, here, is a lousy housewife," joked the second policeman, pointing to the trash on the floor. "I'm Detective Stabler."

Cas stared across the counter. "A young woman came to see you a few hours ago. Where is she?"

"What is all this shit?" Snow rolled his eyes. "I've been here pruning my ass off all morning. The only thing that came to visit was a damn raccoon. Made all this mess. Barbara must have left the back door open."

"You live with someone?"

"Barbara Gelatti. Her family owns the Gelatti vineyards in Sonoma."

"Where is she?"

"Shopping. Oh, wait, I think I hear her car." Snow rose and started to head for the door. Cas stepped in front, blocking his way.

"Cuff this creep and hold onto him," he told the officers. "My fiancée *was* here, in this room. I can smell her perfume."

"You're crazy," snapped Snow. "Barbara wears all that crap. Spends a bloody fortune on it, too."

"Please — cuff him!" insisted Cas, gripping Snow's arm and shoving him towards the policeman.

With a shrug, Benson reached for his handcuffs and locked the suspect's wrists.

"I'll have your badges," Snow screamed. "And you,

whatever your name, I'll have your fucking ass!"

At that moment, a slim woman with thick glasses and straggly hair entered the room, her arms loaded with packages. "My goodness, what's going on?" she asked. "Finn, what are the police doing here?"

"Nothing, Barbara, calm down. These people have just made a big mistake. And I do mean *big*."

"Barbara, my name's Dan Casserly," said Cas, stepping forward. "A young woman came to see your boyfriend this morning and I'm trying to find her. He's conveniently forgotten that she was here."

"Oh, I know she was. I saw her —"

"Barbara's blind as a bat," interrupted Snow, shaking his head sideways. "Can't see her own nose."

"That's mean, Finn." Enjoying the attention, Barbara pretended not to notice his threatening stare. "Just as I was leaving, I saw a girl in a beige Lexus drive up. I love pretty cars. We almost never get visitors, so I assumed she was lost and using our driveway to turn around."

"That's her car," said Cas.

Snow tried to stand up, but Benson held him down. "Damnit, Barbara, you've taken those pills again. You're hallucinating. You don't know what you're talking about."

"I know what I saw, Finn," she whispered, suddenly worried that she'd displeased him.

"Finnegan Snow!" Cas barked, "I'll give you one last chance to save your butt. Where's Hallie?"

"Shove it!"

Struggling for control, Cas turned to the policemen. "Take this lowlife to the station and keep him locked up

219

till I get there. I'm off to search the grounds. Hallie might still be around."

— Chapter 81 —

WITH BARBARA'S HELP, Cas managed to probe every store-room, cabinet and closet where a person might hide or be hidden. Next, he traipsed through the vineyard, peering between bushes and shouting Hallie's name. Discouraged and half-frantic with worry, he stopped for breath at the back door. Suddenly, his phone rang. His voice was tense and anxious. "Yes?"

"Cas — ?" murmured a weak voice.

"Hallie? Oh, God, Hallie, is it you? Are you okay?" He wiped his sweating brow.

"I'm okay," she said weakly. "I'm in my parked car — but don't know where —"

"Can you see out the window?"

"Water – a big lake. A boy lent me his phone. Snow tried to kill me —"

"He can't hurt you now. The police have him. Can you ask the boy the name of the lake?"

"My arm hurts. Wait." She came back a minute later. "Lake Rosalyne — near his house, 234 Harvest Road."

"Stay right where you are. Keep the kid's phone and call me every few minutes. I'm just leaving Snow's house. And don't worry, sweetheart. I'll find you."

It took twenty or so minutes before Cas, with the help of friendly neighbors, found the wooded path to the lake. Hallie's car was parked off the road, about ten feet from the precipice. She was sitting inside, sleepy, but awake.

"I'm getting you to a hospital," he said, helping her out of the car. "Snow must've drugged you. What happened to your arm?"

"Just a bruise. I don't need a doctor. I know what he gave me — or tried to give me."

"Hal, we can't take —"

"I'm okay. Honest! But I don't think I can drive."

He took the cell phone from her hand, added a twenty dollar bill and handed it to the boy standing nearby with his fishing rod. "Thanks, young man, you did a very good deed!"

The lad grinned, grabbed his phone and the money and ran off.

— Chapter 82 —

CAREFUL NOT TO TOUCH anything inside Hallie's car, Cas locked it, made sure Hallie was comfortably seated in his Prius, then phoned the police. Someone from the crime lab, he suggested, should tow Hallie's Lexus to the station and go over it for evidence that Finnegan Snow had been driving it.

En route to the station, Cas again urged Hallie to see a doctor.

"No need," she said, beginning to feel alert again, "You were wonderful to rescue me. My mother saved me, too."

"Oh?"

"When I was young, I had ADHD — Attention-Deficit Hyperactivity Disorder — though I'm not sure there is such a thing. I was just overly active. The teachers favored the slow kids and those of us who knew the lessons got bored and got into mischief."

"Go on."

"My Mom, as you know, is the queen of managing other people's lives and she decided I needed Ritalin. She got her doctor to write a prescription, bought some, gave me a tablet before breakfast and it was horrible! I was even *more* nervous and restless, I was nauseated, I couldn't eat — but she insisted I try it for a few days and 'give it a chance.' "

"Did you?"

"No way! That afternoon, I bought some M&M's. I practiced moving them with my tongue to a safe place in my mouth, swallowed the water, then spit out the candies later. The next morning, I tried the same thing with the Ritalin tablet she gave me, and it worked!"

His eyes widened. "You're telling me —"

"I'm telling you that I got expert at pretending to swallow pills. When Snow gave me two yellow Nembutals, I recognized them from the bottle you found in his bathroom. I did my Ritalin number, but the darn capsules started to dissolve before I could spit them out."

"Two of those pills would've knocked you cold."

"You're so right! Even a little bit made me sleepy. When Snow came back about an hour later, I pretended I was unconscious. He carried me to the car, drove here, put me in the driver's seat with my hands on the wheel, got out and left me rolling towards the water. I had about ten seconds to come alive and stop the car — as you can tell — just in time. Are you sure he's locked up?"

"Yes, you'll see for yourself. If the neighbors' directions are right, we should be at police headquarters in fifteen minutes."

— Chapter 83 —

THE STATION was abuzz with talk and rumors when Hallie and Cas arrived. Snow was in the interrogation room, cuffed, Mirandized and awaiting his lawyer.

Detective Benson seated Hallie and Cas in another room. "I need some history before we start the interview," he told them. "Are you two up to filling me in?"

"We sure are," said Hallie, and launched into a brief summary of what they'd learned, from the time Dale first got them involved to the present.

His tape recorder going, Benson asked numerous questions along the way, and finally said, "Lucky you wear perfume, Ms. Marsh. That's how Mr. Casserly knew you'd been in the house."

She laughed. "But I don't wear perfume. He knows that. I hate the stuff."

"I lied," said Cas.

"Way to go!" Her voice was starting to sound excited. "You know, I had time to think everything over while I was pretending to be knocked out. I've pretty much put together what happened. Want to hear?"

"You have my complete attention," said Benson.

223

"And mine," Cas added.

"I've felt all along that something was staring us in the face and we didn't know what it was," Hallie began. "I don't know why I missed it for so long, but I did. Ever heard of 'midline diastema?' "

"Negative," said Benson.

Cas wrinkled his nose.

"I didn't know the term either, until I found it on Google a few weeks ago. But when Snow tied my hands and went to get a beer, I noticed he first spit something out of his mouth and set it on the sink. It was a retainer — like children wear when they get rid of the bands on their teeth."

"Yeah, my kid had one."

"Right. So I wondered why Snow would be wearing a retainer, then it hit me. He'd had dental work done — dental work to correct the midline diastema — the gap between his two front teeth!"

Cas picked up right away. "You're saying the man who tried to kill you is not Finnegan Snow?"

"That's precisely what I'm saying. Finnegan Snow died in Alaska, probably from an overdose of pentobarbital, better known as Nembutal. The man masquerading as Finnegan Snow is actually his so-called 'best friend,' his brother and his murderer — Shane Snow."

Benson shook his head. "Why would he kill his own brother?"

Hallie smiled. "He was desperate. His world was closing in on him. He was up to his neck in illegal baby trading and he couldn't talk his wife, Jenna, out of writing an exposé. I've a hunch the brothers fought about what to do with Jenna. I don't think Finnegan wanted to kill her."

"But Shane did," said Cas.

"Yes. Shane did what desperate people with no morals do. He made a plan. Since he knew he'd be the obvious suspect in Jenna's death, he decided that Shane should 'die,' too. On that fishing trip to Alaska, Shane poisoned Finnegan, stole his identity and told the world Shane was dead. Then he came home and killed Jenna."

"Whew! Nice guy," commented Cas.

"I'm guessing that one of the first things Shane — as Finnegan — did, was to correct his trademark tooth gap. Then, once he had the death certificate, Shane — parading as Finnegan — went on to collect half the insurance money."

"But he got greedy, right?"

"Right, Cas. He planned to wait the appropriate amount of time, and when Jenna couldn't be found, he'd collect her half, too. In the meantime, he had to get rid of her body and we have proof that he paid to have her cremated."

"What kind of proof?" asked Benson.

"A silver locket that her neighbor and her co-workers say she never took off. It had Shane's picture in it. The man who cremated her thought it might be worth a few bucks in a pawn shop, so he saved it. I bought it from him."

Cas scratched his head. "But if Jenna thought Shane was dead, why was she so secretive about her baby?"

"I'm convinced she still intended to write her exposé. Even if Shane were dead, she knew he was connected to the mobsters working the trade. One of them could easily kill her and steal her baby."

"No wonder she was so protective."

"Once I started putting all this together, I remembered Jenna's notes about Shane's frequent trips to Los Angeles. She suspected he had a partner there and that they were importing infants from other countries, particularly Guatemala. Jenna's neighbor, Birdy, said Jenna told her she was off to L.A. I'd bet anything her 'short trip' was to find out more about his contact."

"Well, young lady," said Benson, standing, "You make one helluva case. I'll need you to sign some papers, then we'll see if we can get this dirtbag to talk."

Hallie frowned. "Are you sure you have enough evidence to hold him? I'd hate to think he could get out on bail."

Benson shook his head. "Never happen. After we check your story, we can charge him with two counts of murder, one count of attempted murder, insurance fraud, larceny, burglary, perjury, identity theft...he's going away for a long, long time. I'll talk to your Frisco D.A. about how we handle this. You'll be around to testify?"

"You bet! And thanks so much for all your help."

The officer turned to Cas. "You've got one hell of a smart lady there. I wouldn't want her coming after me."

Cas grinned. "Don't worry, detective. From now on, she'll be on a very short leash."

— Chapter 84 —

EN ROUTE back to San Francisco that evening, Hallie nestled up against the driver. "Did I mention how grateful I am that you came after me this morning?" she asked, not waiting for a reply. "But what's this nonsense about a short leash?"

"Figuratively speaking, my sweet. I almost lost you today. You took a very foolish chance. Do you realize how close you came to being killed?"

"Of course I do. I'd never forgive myself if that monster had killed me."

"It's nothing to joke about. I know you love to play detective and you're wonderful at gathering facts and piecing them together, but sometimes..."

"No lectures, please? You did get a great story and an exclusive — will you write about it?"

"Not everything. But I'll finish Jenna's exposé of black market baby brokers, tie it in with her disappearance and how the police solved her murder. I'll leave out Dale, Birdy and Vicky."

"And me."

"Precisely. You don't need to tell the world — particularly your mother — how close you came to an early demise."

"You're right, as aways." She snuggled closer.

"Thanks for calling Sara and telling her all's well. She's got her big dinner with Dale tonight. Do you think he'll propose?"

"On their first date?"

"Why not? I lent her that sexy blue dress you like. I remember wearing it to dinner one night and you couldn't wait to tear it off me."

"As I recall," he said, "you took it off yourself, hung it up very carefully, slipped into your nightie and crawled in the sack with me."

"Picky, picky. Why do you have to have such a good memory?" She kissed his cheek. "Anyway, I promise I'll be more careful the next time we have a mystery to solve."

"The only mystery we're going to solve," he said, "is how I'm going to keep you out of trouble."

She laughed happily. "Yes, my love, that *may* be a problem."

— Chapter 85 —

DALE PULLED up to Sara's apartment and miracle of miracles, found a space right in front. "The parking God is with me," he murmured, glancing at his watch. Five minutes early — he'd better stay in the car. If Sara was anything like Daisy, she'd keep him waiting half an hour. Fortunately, Sara was nothing like Daisy.

Sitting there anxiously, Dale's mind raced back to Cas's earlier phone call. Thanks to Hallie's dogged sleuthing and Cas's investigative skills, Jenna's disappearance was no longer a mystery. The clues had come together, the perpetrator was caught, the case was solved. Only a few loose ends remained.

At seven prompt, Dale rang the doorbell. Sara answered — an angel, he thought, in a pale blue dress that showed her gentle curves. Her only jewelry was a thin gold necklace.

Momentarily speechless, Dale finally murmured, "You — look spectacular."

"Thanks," she said, smiling. "It's Hallie's dress. She insisted I try to look nice for you."

"Nice isn't the word!"

"Well, actually, the word she used was 'seductive.' "

He swallowed hard. "If you looked any more seductive, we'd never get to dinner. Ready to go?"

"Yes, unless you'd like a cocktail."

"No, thanks," he said, "better bring a coat."

— Chapter 86 —

GIOIA D'ITALIA, a popular North Beach bistro, was small and dark, but the food was Italian, not French, the candles were lit by batteries and the "romantic" music was Verdi's thumping Anvil Chorus.

Hallie would not approve, thought Sara, grateful that Dale hadn't taken her to a fancy restaurant with tiny portions and huge prices.

He followed behind her, squeezing into a corner booth.

"Signore Redington," announced a waiter, appearing suddenly, "*e che bella signorina*! Welcome to Gioia d'Italia."

"Grazie, Gino."

The man set down a gold-labeled bottle. Sara looked to Dale. "We don't need champagne," she whispered.

"Yes, we do." He motioned to Gino to pop the cork. "We're celebrating our first date."

"In that case, let's drink to your amazing recovery. No one could possibly imagine what you've been through."

"Fate did me a favor," he said softly. "If I hadn't been burned, I wouldn't have met you. We can also celebrate Hallie and Cas and their capture of the Terrible Mr. Snow."

"Poor Hallie. What a horrible experience."

"She's rather impulsive, isn't she?"

"Patience isn't her strong point."

"If you hadn't been smart enough to call Cas, and he hadn't gone after her, Snow might've gone back to finish the job. Speaking of jobs, I got a call from my Dad today. He said he realized I was never happy working in the business office; he offered me a new job heading the family foundation."

"Sounds perfect for you. Congratulations!"

"Thanks, I'm delighted. We meet next week to make final decisions for the year. I'll enjoy giving grants to worthy causes."

"I got a call today, too, from my pal Genelle at the hospital. The latest is that a large group of female staffers got together to sue Mitch for sexual harassment. They were all willing to testify and he'd have lost his license, for sure. But the families of Mitch's patients pleaded with them not to take him to court. Their relatives all had surgeries scheduled and they were counting on Mitch —"

"That's the sad part. He is a gifted surgeon."

"Yes, the nurses admitted that. They went back and forth and finally voted to send a letter to Mitch and a copy to the head of the Medical Staff signed by twenty-two women. They explained the situation and decided to give Mitch one more chance. But if he so much as *winks* at a female on hospital grounds, they'll take him to court."

"Good for them! I wonder if Daisy heard about that."

"According to Genelle, Mitch tried to dump Daisy by telephone. She was furious, went to his apartment that evening and found him with some woman. He came to work the next day sporting a big black eye."

"Too bad she didn't aim lower."

Sara smiled. "I think that romance is over."

"Speaking of romance..." He set down his glass and spoke with quiet intensity. "You must know I'm out of my mind in love with you, Sara. You're in my every thought, my every wish, my every dream. I'm not good at this and I can't get down on my knees, but Sara Bowman, I love you, I adore you, I can't live without you. Will you do me the honor of becoming my wife and letting me spend the rest of my days making you happy?"

Tears flooded her eyes. "Dale — I love you so much," she said and gently kissed his lips. "I think I first fell in love with you when Jimmy told you I was fifty and frumpy. It didn't change anything. You were the same kind, modest man and so incredibly brave. But how will your son —"

"Jimmy's way ahead of us. He's already texted me that I should 'hook up' with you before some 'cool dude' comes along and steals you."

"He's a terrific young man. And — Vicky? Have you called Birdy?"

"No, I'll call her tomorrow. You liked Vicky, didn't you?"

"How could I not like her? She's a sweet, adorable baby."

"She just had her first birthday. It's time she found a real home. Sara — we could be wonderful parents to little Vicky…"

"I confess that thought crossed my mind."

"I've a confession, too. My lawyer's already preparing adoption papers."

She laughed. "I guess you were pretty sure of me. Could Birdy be her nanny till she gets used to us?"

"She'll be thrilled."

"And what will we do when Vicky starts asking questions?"

"Mark Twain said, 'When in doubt, tell the truth.' We'll simply explain that her mother went to Heaven and we were lucky enough to be able to make her *our* daughter. We'll tell her the rest when she's old enough to handle it. But you haven't answered my — um, big question."

"I almost have. First, my brother Roger has to check you out."

Dale's eyes widened. "Oh? What do I have to do to get his approval?"

"Nothing, really. He's so anxious to get me married

off, he'd approve of a cockroach."

"How flattering."

"But I like you better." She smiled and took both his hands in hers. "I'd love to marry you, Mr. Redington, and be the mother of your — well, actually — somebody else's child. I can never resist a twofer. But before I say yes, there's something you should know about me."

"You're addicted to Snickers bars"

"Nope."

"You love to gamble."

"Nope."

"You cheated on your last drivers' license test?"

"Nope."

"I give up."

She leaned into his ear. "I snore — and loudly! My brother Gary taped me once. You could hear me all the way downstairs in the living room."

He burst into laughter. "In that case, we're *both* going to need ear plugs. Anything else about you I should know?"

"Just one. My family will adore you. You'll love my Mom and my younger brothers, but Roger, I guess I better tell you — he's handsome, he's brilliant, he's charming, but — he's a sex maniac."

Dale groaned and heaved a sigh. "Sara, darling, are you very hungry?

"Not really."

"Could you live with a frozen pizza? Later?"

"I live on frozen pizzas."

"Thank you, God. Gino!" he called, reaching for her

coat, "would you please bring me the check?"

***

LaVergne, TN USA
18 February 2011
217022LV00001B/1/P